VULTURE VALLEY

VULTURE VALLEY

TOM WEST

CUTTING EDGE

ISBN-13: 978-1-954840-43-0

Published by
Cutting Edge Books
PO Box 8212
Calabasas, CA 91372
www.cuttingedgebooks.com

CHAPTER ONE

H AP HARRIGAN had a belligerent jaw, but there was little else belligerent about him when two guards packed him out of the Snake Pen and dumped his battered form onto the rock floor of Cell 2. They dumped him as carelessly as though they were handling a sack of garbage — and with as much distaste.

He lay where they had dropped him, just inside the iron-bound door, a young man not yet out of his twenties, rough-hewn features dyed deep by the desert sun and legs bowed from the saddle. Above his rope-scarred hands the wrists were blue-wealed by the shackles. Dried blood rusted his unruly blond hair and clotted his smashed nose. Faint indentations at the corners of his stubborn mouth told of laughter wrinkles that three months in Yuma had almost erased. Three months — and his sentence was twelve years!

A grey scab blotched on a granite bluff, around which lapped the sullen waters of the yellow Colorado, the Arizona Territorial Penitentiary smouldered beneath a brassy sun that bit like a branding iron. Behind its thick adobe walls men festered in tight-packed rock-and-adobe cells, rotted in dungeons hewn from the solid rock, or raved in the Snake Pen, a cave tunnelled deep into the bowels of the earth, where eternal silence absorbed the screams of shackled men and grisly demons of insanity stalked the darkness.

No hombre was too tough for Yuma to tame!

Weathered redwood markers, row upon row, in the cemetery outside the massive walls told of those who had sought freedom and found release — cut down by the blast of a guard's shot-gun, or drowned in the swirling, silt-laden river. Around, an arid expanse of desert stretched to the haze of the horizon, a waste of sand and cactus, scoured by bands of wandering Conopahs and Yumas, ever alert for sight of a sun-seared, exhausted fugitive whose capture and return meant fifty dollars bounty — affluence for a desert Indian.

Stretched on the straw pallets of their bunks, the five other convicts who packed the narrow cell eyed Harrigan's sprawled form with no expression in their bleak eyes save heat-ridden boredom. Brutality meant nothing to these case-hardened desperados. Men calloused by killings could not be expected to blink at a beating.

The iron-bound door slammed shut on gritty hinges and a bolt rasped into place. There was silence in the stifling rock-and-adobe cell — three bunks to a side and a narrow alleyway between, exact counterpart of thirty-three other cells in the main block — a silence that reflected the apathetic indifference of its inmates.

Butch, bull-necked, with bloodshot eyes, sweating out fifteen years for a stage holdup and killing, finally yawned and grunted, with a nod towards the bloodied form by the doorway, "Kin yuh beat thet! Sixty days in the Snake Pen and he come out alive. Wal, they sure worked him over plenty!"

Drago, veteran of a dozen holdups, bared yellow teeth in a silent grin, "What did the lunkhead expect, conkin' a guard with a shovel — and f'r no reason at all!"

"Reckon they beat out what little brains he had," threw in Lerew, the knifer, a mixed blood with high cheek bones and beady eyes.

"It is hard for those who kick against the pricks of outrageous fortune, but despair is a potent goad, gentlemen!" The words rolled out as though from a pulpit, deep-voiced and melodious.

"Aw, quit dribbling, Slick!" snarled Lerew, "Thet jackass don't know sic-em!"

The convict dubbed Slick Sam dangled long legs over the edge of his bunk and dropped to the floor. He was a rawboned, powerfully built fellow, with a jaw like a rock-crusher. Deepset above a hawk nose, his piercing dark eyes regarded the figure sprawled on the cell's threshold. Of the five, his face alone reflected no brutality. His forehead was lofty, mouth firm and intelligent. The prison records tallied him as confidence man, card shark and gunman, convicted of robbery with violence. They also revealed that he was graduate of a famous college, from a distinguished family. But the devil had dabbled with his destiny. A strange man, devious and dangerous — kingpin of Cell 2.

Musing, Sam scanned Hap Harrigan's loose-limbed form. "Hot young colts, being raged, do rage the more!" he murmured. Turning, dark eyes gleaming with cynical amusement, he added, melodiously, "Shakespeare, gentlemen!"

"Aw, go jump in the river!" snapped Lerew.

The battered young convict's eyelids flicked up and two smouldering blue eyes, dull with hopelessness, focussed Sam's burly form.

"You are indeed fortunate, brother, to be alive," intoned the big man. "The hounds who guard such as we resent violence, except, of course, on their own part. You are a marked man, brother. They will kill you next time."

"The quicker the better," came back Harrigan hoarsely.

"You have transgressed, brother, a killing I believe," continued Slick equably. "The way of the transgressor is hard." He swung around, "From the Scriptures, you should explore the territory, gentlemen!" He turned back to the prone man, "Now you must pay in sweat and suffering."

Harrigan struggled to a sitting position, propped his aching body against the door. He was lanky and loose-jointed. His eyes, cooler now, were wide-set and steady, with the glint of steel in their challenging directness.

"Sure, that goes — for you jaspers." His voice was heavy with weariness. "You got it coming. Me — I was framed — some skunk bushwhacked my pard and they put the finger on me."

Lerew's laugh grated. "D'ye hear the young buck? Framed! Hell, warn't we all framed?"

"Me, too," chuckled Butch thickly.

"Into your bunk and rest, brother!" directed Slick, still standing above Harrigan. "You'll be for the rock pile at sunup."

The young rider attempted to rise, sank back against the door with a groan. "Aw, what's the use?" he muttered.

Without further word, Slick bent, gathered up the lean form and, without apparent effort, laid the battered Harrigan in a lower bunk. Eyes thoughtful, he hunkered beside it.

Beyond the adobe walls that ringed the penitentiary, a full sixteen inches thick, the sun dropped low across the desert. Through the small barred aperture that admitted scant air and little light, a crimson sword thrust into the graying cell.

"Though your sins be scarlet, they shall be as white as snow," murmured Slick.

"I ain't sinned, none to speak of," reiterated the young convict in the bunk.

"Thou shalt not kill!"

"I never killed nobody!" Gnawing memories brittled Harrigan's pain-weary voice.

"You as good as staked a claim on boothill, pard," came Butch's husky tones from the top bunk, "when you conked thet guard. They don't stand for no shenanigans in Yuma."

"Reckless youth makes rueful age," murmured Slick. Suddenly his head swivelled and his square jaw thrust into the bunk, "Would you be free, brother?" he inquired softly.

Harrigan groaned from sheer anguish of spirit. "For Gawd's sake, quit, Sam. I'm in no mood f'r funning."

"This is no jest. I, too, am weary of this devil's dumping ground. A hunch has come to me, brother, that may set us outside the walls. Would you take a chance, a desperate chance?"

The bloodied Harrigan was up on an elbow now, staring fixedly at Slick Sam's hawklike features. "Chance!" His bruised lips quirked into a grin that held no humor, "Heck, ain't I branded f'r boothill? Deal the hand — any hand — and I'll play it."

Slick turned away and eyed the slit of darkening sky visible through the narrow window. Half to himself, he muttered, "Cloudy and little moon. Maybe the Gods will smile — and maybe they will laugh!"

His attention focussed again upon Harrigan's intent features, "Listen, brother!" For awhile he spoke in subdued tones, then straightened, stretched like a great bear and climbed nimbly into his bunk above.

Night threw a merciful cloak over the penitentiary. Atop the main tower that rose square beside the entrance a guard moved restlessly beside the multi-barrelled Gatling machine gun that thrust its steel snout through the notched wall, ready to spray the prison yard below with leaden hail. Pacing to ease cramped legs, the guard glanced longingly at the flaring lights of town, strewn across the flats and sandhills west of the prison. The faint low roar that pulsated through the still air spoke tantalizingly of high life in Yuma — of crowded saloons, painted women, jostling humanity, excitement, companionship; for Yuma was in its heydey, the raw, lusty metropolis of the southwest.

Supplies for military posts, mines, trading posts were stacked high in its warehouses. Here, too, the wagon trains of immigrants, heading for California, were ferried across the river. Merchants, prospectors, gamblers, adventurers, Indians thronged its plankwalks and packed its bawdy houses. This was the artery through which blood flowed into the veins of the raw, awakening southwest. Above and beyond this uproarious conglomeration of warehouses, wagons and wantons towered the grim penitentiary.

Wide-eyed in the darkness of the cell, Hap Harrigan battled despair. He knew now why any wild creature, whether it was gray wolf, snarling panther or slim-legged antelope, wilted and died when it was caged; he knew the utter hopelessness of a man who sees death, cold and inevitable, close ahead; he knew the bitterness that could sear the soul of a man imprisoned for a crime he did not commit. Thought of Sam's words drifted into his mind, the hopeless escape scheme of the confidence man who quoted Scripture like a preacher and faced life with a bland serenity that even Yuma could not disturb. Well, he reflected somberly, better die in a swift smash for freedom than wait to have his brains beaten out in the black horror of the Snake Pen.

He lay slack, sick in mind and body, the heavy breathing of his cellmates upon his ears, when a sibilant hiss from the bunk above aroused him to alert attention.

"Harrigan, you ready?"

"Rarin' to go!" he whispered.

"Then turn it on! 'Who has lost his freedom has nothing else to lose.' "

Harrigan commenced to mutter, quietly at first, then louder, louder. His limbs jerked. He writhed and moaned. His wild delirium filled the cell.

Drago's wheezing ceased. His irate voice came across the cell, "F'r gosh sakes, button up!" Curses and threats from other disturbed sleepers punched through the darkness. But Harrigan groaned the more.

"Quiet!" roared Slick. "Have you no hearts, you scorpions? The man's delirious, maybe dying." His bulk showed shadowy beside Hap's bunk as he slid down and bent over the squirming form, "Taper it off!" he whispered urgently, "Time you checked out!"

Gradually the moaning died down, ceased. Relieved oaths sparked from the bunks around. Then Slick's grave tones, deep with concern, flowed through the gloom, "Harrigan's dead, gentlemen! To die quickly is sometimes a privilege. I knew his brain was injured."

"I said they worked the bustard over plenty," grunted Butch.

"I'd have throttled the mulehead anyways, ef he hadn't quit," came Lerew's acrid tones. "Mebbe we'll get some shuteye now!"

"Sleep, with a dead man in the cell!" Sam's deep voice dripped distaste. "No, siree, I want that stiff out of here." With that, he raised his voice, bellowing like a bull and banging the door with his fists, "Guard, Guard!"

Boots scraped the rock outside. The door squealed open and a uniformed guard stood framed in the doorway, a double-barrelled shotgun slanted in his hands as he peered cautiously into the darkened cell. Behind him, another guard held a smoking stable lantern shoulder high with one hand and fingered the butt of a holstered six-gun with the other. The feeble glow of the lantern yellowed the faces of the convicts raising up in their bunks, showed Sam's burly form jammed in the alleyway.

"What's the trouble?" demanded the guard with the shotgun, eyes alert with suspicion.

"Harrigan's dead. He died in delirium, a head injury I would say," returned Sam, voice low and solemn, "May the Lord have mercy upon his soul!"

"The loco puncher," threw in the guard with the lantern. "Maybe Jim handled the lobo too rough, he beaned his brother." He sighed resignedly, "Guess we gotta pack him to the death house. Betcher he weighs one-sixty."

"From the dust we came and to the dust shall we return," intoned Sam. "I will convey this poor clay to the mortuary, gentlemen. 'Tis the last sad office for a friend." Without waiting for the guards' assent, he reached into the bunk where Harrigan lay with closed eyes. As his head and shoulders emerged and he straightened, cradling the limp form, Harrigan's head fell backward and his jaw dropped slackly.

Slowly, solemnly, Sam paced to the door. The guards stood aside. One slammed the door behind him and secured it; the other led the way with his lantern. A melancholy procession, they trudged across the prison yard, the shotgun guard bringing up the rear.

As they moved, Sam's keen eyes probed his surroundings in the uncertain light. Ahead, dark-limned against the night, rose the main guard tower, close by the great timbered gates. To its right bulked the guards' quarters, square shafts of light from the windows patching the ground outside. Beyond was the mortuary.

Midway across the yard a squat, rectangular building was set — the bathhouse, casting a long shadow across the smooth-swept ground.

It was plain that they would pass through that shadow, swiftly considered Sam, and it was the only spot until they entered the mortuary, dangerously close to the guards' quarters, where they would be shielded from the scrutiny of the guard atop the watch tower.

The blotch of shadow enveloped them. Sam stumbled, fell.

He struggled weakly to his feet, swayed uncertainly above Harrigan's form, flopped loosely on the ground, then staggered back toward the guard with the shotgun. "My heart!" he gasped. "Another attack! I should have known better." Choking, right hand clamped against his chest, he tottered closer to the shotgun.

"Aw, hell!" grumbled the guard with the lantern, a short, muscular fellow. He stepped carelessly across Harrigan's prone form, extended the lantern to his companion, "Guess I gotta pack the stiff. Grab this, Pete!"

Harrigan, lying upon his back, was closely following the play through slitted eyes. In a flash, he saw Slick Sam explode into action. Slick's knotted right fist pistoned into the squat guard's jaw. The lantern crashed to the ground, its glass funnel splintering into fragments. While the guard still tettered, out on his feet, Sam pivoted and leapt. Like a panther, he was atop the shotgun guard and smothering him before the fellow realized his intent. One brawny arm circled the guard's neck, the hand clamping over mouth and nose, muffling the yell in his throat. Sam's other hand gripped the barrel of the gun, twisting. The shotgun dropped with a clatter. Prisoner and guard went down in a grunting, threshing flurry.

Harrigan scrambled to his feet. The squat guard had dropped, as stiff as a ramrod, and the flame of the lantern petered out beside him. Harrigan stooped over him, quickly unbuckled his gunbelt and swung it around his own waist. Grabbing the gun butt, he sprang towards the interlocked forms of Sam and the remaining gaurd. But Sam had done his job. He shook himself free of the guard's limp arms, rose and scanned the darkened yard. Nothing moved. "Quick!" he ejaculated, "Into their uniforms!" And he commenced stripping the man at his feet.... Two unconscious men, naked except for under-drawers and booted feet, bound and gagged with strips of their shirts, were bundled against the rough adobe of the bathhouse wall.

Panting from their exertions, the two prisoners wriggled into uniforms that refused to fit. Sam strove vainly to button a tunic across his broad chest, while Harrigan surveyed serge pants that left his legs exposed to the calves. But never a gunbelt felt more comfortable than that which held the holstered .45 he had buckled around his waist.

Sam abandoned attempts to button the tunic, picked up the shotgun.

"What's next?" demanded Harrigan, a new vibrancy in his voice.

Sam hefted the shotgun, "Bloody death or freedom, brother, and either fast! Listen! The guard atop the tower doubtless saw us cross the yard. Three men passed behind this bathhouse, two will emerge. If he challenges, rush the gate. Our gamble is that he may mistake us for guards and be satisfied. Are you ready? Slowly now!"

Shoulder to shoulder, they stepped out into the wan moonlight.

CHAPTER TWO

EVERY NERVE TAUT as a fiddlestring, Harrigan stepped beside the slow-pacing Sam. Mastering a panicky impulse to rush madly for the gates, he tried to control his racing pulse and to forget that, at any moment, a stream of hot lead from the machine gun atop the tower might mow them down.

But no sharp-voiced challenge cut through the night. At that moment the guard was wistfully eying the lights of town, debating whether it would not be wiser to trade his dreary round in Yuma for an outside job, a river boat maybe, or a freighting outfit.

Each measured step brought the pair closer to the great gates, closed and barred. Harrigan's pulse redoubled its pounding when he glimpsed a small rectangular door, large enough to allow the passage of a man, cut out of the right-hand gate. It was ajar. Not half a dozen paces from it, an oil lamp, bracketed on the wall of the adjacent guards' quarters, threw a pallid circle of light. Then his heart suddenly flip-flopped. Nodding on a bench below the light was another guard. A Sharps was propped against the wall beside him and his tunic was loosened against the closeness of the night.

At sound of their footsteps, plain on the rocky ground, the guard's head came up with a jerk. It swivelled in their direction, his glance ran over them, then his chin dropped down again upon his chest. The released breath whistled between Hap's lips. Sweat trickled below the stiff-rimmed uniform cap. Another dozen paces and they would be outside. The incredible had happened.

Slick Sam's crazy scheme had worked — they were walking out of Yuma. Then the Gods laughed!

Something had registered in the gatekeeper's mind, sleepy as he was, a false note that aroused his suspicions. Maybe he had glimpsed Harrigan's bare ankles or perhaps Sam's loose-hanging tunic. His drowsiness dropped from him. With a sharp exclamation he was on his feet, reaching for the Sharps.

Harrigan plunged for the small doorway like a spurred pony, but Slick was before him. The big man hurled his bulk in the direction of the guard. Too startled to shout, the latter swung up the Sharps. Before he could squeeze the trigger, Sam was upon him. One arm swept aside the barrel, the other grabbed the guard's throat. The shell exploded with a roar that seemed to Harrigan, now racing at Sam's heels, like a thunderclap of fate.

"The gate!" panted Sam, flinging the guard against the wall.

Harrigan dove for the postern, conscious that more guards, some in shirtsleeves, others hastily buttoning tunics, were spilling through the doorway of the building on his right. Flame stabbed the gloom. A slug whined past and embedded itself in the timbers of the gate. Then he dove through the opening, Sam panting at his heels.

Outside, his companion checked, whirled. Twice the shotgun roared as he emptied both barrels through the open postern, into the smudge of moving bodies that were the guards stampeding in pursuit. Gunfire lashed back. Sam flung the shotgun aside and swung around to Harrigan. "Adios, brother — it is each man for himself and the devil take the hindmost!" With that, he was lost in the night.

For an instant, Harrigan stood irresolute, senses awhirl with excitement. Above him towered the great gates and the square guard tower. Inside the gates he could hear shouting and trampling of feet, but the shotgun blast had checked immediate pursuit.

A great bell inside the prison began to clang, slowly and ponderously. The deep menacing note of its bronze tongue reverberated through the town, across the river, out into the desert, carrying the tidings of a prison break.

To Harrigan the pulsating waves of sound were like notes of a funeral dirge. The break was no secret now. He was a fugitive, to be hunted down and shot like a coyote. The guards would kill him with no more compunction than they would gun a mad dog. Every man's hand would be against him.

Panic flooded the fugitive. He hesitated no longer. Like a deer, he raced frantically along in the shadow of the prison wall, stumbling over uneven ground, breaking through straggling brush, leaping boulders, oblivious of thorny branches that ripped his clothing and tore his flesh. No thought possessed him but an obsession to leave the prison gates behind and get away from that tolling bell.

Crouching low, he swerved from the wall that rose black above him and headed out into the open, and blessed the clouds that blanketed a small segment of moon. Beating through scrubby brush, scrambling up and down sandy swales, circling bare patches, he scurried across the waste like the hunted animal he was. Finally, gulping great breaths of the night air, he sank down exhausted.

His breathing less labored, he raised off the ground and looked behind. Lanterns swarmed like fireflies around the main gates. The great bell still tolled on like a pendulum of doom. Self-control was flowing back now and the fugitive's mind began to function normally. He cudgelled his brains, trying to frame a plan of escape. Where was Slick Sam heading? Chances were, he thought, with a touch of envy, Sam had every move figured before he left the cell.

He had achieved the freedom for which he yearned, considered the fugitive grimly, now what was he going to do with it? Trouble was, he felt as confused as a colt in a strange corral.

Somewhere behind him flowed the broad Colorado, cutting off escape to the east. The ferry would be watched. Quickly, he rejected the idea of stealing a boat and floating downstream. He was a plainsman, with an instinctive distrust of the great yellow Colorado. The desert was wide and stretched to the Border, but he knew it offered nothing but death to a man afoot, with no food or water and no knowledge of its waterholes. There remained the town. Harrigan fingered his ill-fitting guard's uniform, torn and stained in his wild plunging through the brush. He'd make a pretty sight in town. First thing to do was to shuck this rig.

He rose to his feet and moved forward again, more slowly now, working towards the lights of town. Before dawn he had to ditch the giveaway guard's uniform and find a place of concealment.

The mesquite thinned out and he drifted like a shadow across the silent sand hills. A dog yapped sharply and sweat ran cold down his backbone as he avoided a darkened shack. The ground firmed and he stood on a road that snaked away into the night. He paused, debating, quickly flattened at the squeal of a dry hub and a bullwhacker's blistering accents. A huge freight wagon ground out of the gloom, swaying with its creaking load behind a twenty mule team. The bullwhacker's whip cracked and sulphurous expletives exploded like firecrackers, as he tooled a jerk-line team through the night.

The fugitive's lips quirked as the great wheels ground by. This was a breath of better days. For the first time a wave of confidence swept over him. This was where he belonged. He straightened and swung up behind the wagon, clambered over the end-gate and scrambled atop the load. Flattened upon a roped bale, he lay relaxed as the wagon crawled in the direction of town.

The lead mule wheeled through the wide gateway of a wagon yard, flanked by long storage sheds. Harrigan dropped off. He was on the outskirts of town now. Around him, shacks, adobes and warehouses were strewn helter-skelter. A few hundred paces up the wide road two kerosene flares blazed outside a barnlike structure. Ponies were tied to the hitch-rail outside. Nervously alert, the fugitive sidled towards it, gained the friendly darkness of an alley beside the saloon. From his hiding place he watched the batwings. High-booted teamsters, alkalied prospectors and spurred riders banged in and out. The drone of deep voices flowed to his ears, punctuated by an occasional exuberant shout, the crash of a broken bottle, the tinkle of glasses. Harrigan sucked his dry lips, never had he craved a drink more, or stood less chance of getting it. His muscles tensed. A booze-muddled puncher, wide-brimmed Stetson askew, leather chaps flapping and knotted bandanna awry, stumbled out and waved towards the angle of the building behind which the fugitive crouched.

Harrigan's fist took him beside the jaw as he breasted the mouth of the alley. He went down like a pole-axed steer. Harrigan grabbed him under the armpits and dragged him back into the gloom of the alley.

"I hate to do this, feller," he murmured, as he commenced to strip off the inert puncher's plaid shirt, "but I'm in no position to be finicky."

Features shaded by the down-tilted brim of the Stetson, spur chains clinking and a wild excitement pulsing through his body, the fugitive jingled beneath the canopies of Main Street. Feel of the familiar range garb and the infectious glamor of the life that whirled around him instilled in him a vast content. But reason told him he was walking on a razor's edge.

This was a salty town, he decided. A surging throng jammed the plankwalks and spilled out into the rutted street. Flares blazed before the false fronts of saloons, gambling houses and dance halls, jostling each other like painted jades. Sober-clad business men rubbed elbows with blanket-swathed Indians; spruce cavalrymen pushed past velvet-clad Mexican vaqueros; bearded bullwhackers shouldered pale-faced gamblers. Shouts of brawling men, the shrill laughter of hardeyed women, the monotonous chant of barkers, beat upon his ears in a confused roar, while the continuous thud of booted feet upon the hollow plankwalks provided a rumbling monotone.

The dreary penitentiary seemed as remote as the moon itself. This was another world. Already his prison memories were fading like a forgotten nightmare.

He hesitated outside a saloon, battling a consuming thirst. There was safety in a crowd, he reasoned, and shouldered through a press of prospectors, teamsters and Mexicans into the buzzing beehive behind the batwings. Perspiring bartenders were pushing drinks across a long plank bar lined two-deep with patrons. Men bunched around tables dotted across the sawdust-covered floor and thronged the gambling tables.

Elbowing to the bar, the fugitive paid for a bottle of bourbon from the roll he had discovered in the puncher's pants pocket and carried it to a table against the wall. There he sat and sipped slowly, savoring every drop of the fiery liquor and luxuriating in his newfound freedom, senses feasting on the roar of life around.

A dance hall in the rear was jampacked with swirling couples, short-skirted women and sweating men. The scraping of the fiddles made heavenly music in his ears. The stench of sweat and spilled booze and rank tobacco poisoned the air. But the fugitive breathed deep — to him it was ambrosia.

He rolled a smoke and his glance fell on the crowded gambling tables beyond him, where men were lavishly staking their dinero upon chuck-a-luck, faro and blackjack. He fingered the roll in his pocket. Fed by the bourbon and the exhilaration of freedom, a surge of confidence swept over him. He sauntered to the nearest table, ringed with blackjack players. His glance dropped incuriously upon the sober-clad dealer — and every muscle in his body became rigid. He was looking at the sallow features of Cheyenne Dan, the gambler whose perjured evidence had condemned him to Yuma.

As though the bitterness that boiled in the fugitive's tight-focussed eyes had bored through to his consciousness, the gambler's low-lidded eyes, expressionless as glass beads, raised from the table. Incredulity clouded them. Then recollection, perhaps remembrance of the tolling of the prison bell, flashed into their pale depths. The thin lips twitched beneath the waxed mustache. The gambler's right hand slipped quickly beneath his black coat. Harrigan's six-gun roared as Cheyenne flicked out a stubby derringer.

A crimson stain spread swiftly over the front of the gambler's white shirt. Blood splashed upon the liquor-stained card table as he slumped across it. Chairs crashed as men flung away. The drone of voices was chopped off, succeeded by a brittle expectancy. Harrigan, death in his cold blue eyes, backed towards the batwings and men shrank before the menace of his smoking gun. Gaining the street, he wormed through the swirling throng. The mood of elation had evaporated. Once again he was a hunted animal. Hurrying he knew not where, he found himself abreast a lot beside a livery barn. It was darkened and deserted, save for wagons lined up on either side and tethered lines of mules, munching piled hay.

Weariness seized upon the fugitive. He felt exhausted, physically and mentally. Frayed nerves and aching muscles craved rest. He slid down the line of wagons with their bulging canvas tops, crawled beneath one at random and quickly dropped into the deep sleep of exhaustion.

The cursing of teamsters, rattle of harness, rumble of iron-rimmed wheels stirred him into wakefulness. Limbs stiff with the chill of a desert dawn, he sat up drowsily and blinked into grayness between the spokes of a wheel. The wagons were pulling out. Already several unwieldy Merivales were lurching down street. Then the wagon bed above him quivered, moved.

Fully awake now, Harrigan glanced ahead — and saw the straining legs of a six-mule team as the animals set their weight on the traces. A whip cracked and the wagon rolled forward. As the cooney scraped his head, the fugitive gathered himself together, jumped to his feet, pushed aside the canvas curtain draped across the rear of the wagon and dove headlong inside.

For awhile, he lay in the semi-darkness, cursing himself for a bonehead. By sheer good luck alone had the wagon been unoccupied. At that, he had no notion where he was headed.

He peered cautiously out across the end-gate. More wagons were trailing behind, coiling down a sandy road that led riverward.

As the light strengthened, he examined the interior of the Conestoga curiously. Two bedrolls were spooled and roped, and a pile of bundles were stacked in the forefront. Pots and pans rattled and a large hinged box plainly held chuck. A man's jeans and several woman's long dresses dangled from a bow. Man and wife, he decided.

Brakes squealed and the wagon jerked to an abrupt stop, almost throwing him off his feet. He picked his way forward, parted the canvas that hid the driver a mite and peered ahead, past the broad back of the man on the seat. In front, other wagons were lined up, down to a flat jetty at the river's edge, against which a ponderous, pontoon-like barge was moored. Two wagons were already on the barge and a third was halted on the jetty. But what took his eye and brought the cold sweat of fear was three armed guards carefully inspecting the wagon on the jetty. In a flash, the fugitive grasped the peril of his position. The hunt was on. This was the ferry across the Colorado and prison guards were searching every vehicle that crossed.

Quickly, he stepped back to the tail of the wagon again, mind in a ferment. Behind were a string of halted wagons, on either side bare sandhills. To his left, the penitentiary sat upon its granite bluff, massive and somber. More guards were moving through the patched brush where he had so blindly scrambled the night before, beating every bush.

The fugitive's stomach shrank into a cold knot. The paralyzing panic of a cornered animal gripped him. Instinctively, his right hand touched the butt of the holstered .45. He stiffened. Lips tight set, he worked up the wagon bed again.

Thrusting the curtains aside, he jabbed the muzzle of the six-gun into the small of the driver's back. "One peep, mister," he warned softly, "and you're buzzard bait."

Beyond a spasmodic quiver of shock, the black-coated man in the stiff-brimmed Stetson who held the lines gave no sign. Motionless, he stared straight ahead.

Then Harrigan glimpsed the girl beside him, thick-clustered curls straying beneath her poke bonnet. She was gazing at a stern-wheeler churning up stream, unaware of the intruder behind her.

"Move over a mite, ma'am!" requested Harrigan politely.

At sound of his voice, she jumped with surprise, stifling a startled shriek. Her head swivelled and her lips parted in a gasp of amazement at sight of the fugitive's grim, unshaven features and the gun pressed into the heavy-set driver's back.

"Bottle up, ma'am!" advised Harrigan tightly, "That is ef you don't crave to bury your husband."

"It's my dad!" she ejaculated. "And who are you, to hold up honest folks in broad daylight?"

"Escaped convict, ma'am," came back the fugitive curtly.

"Figured you was the feller the sheriff's hot after for a saloon shooting last night," put in the driver, without turning his head.

"I am," said Harrigan shortly. "It's death if they take me — another killing won't make no difference. You're looking right into the Golden Gates, mister." As he spoke, his mind registered that he had never seen a prettier girl, despite the lines of indignation that fretted her forehead. Her face was oval and sun-tanned, her lips firm and eyes as cool and clear as the waters of a mountain lake. She seemed more riled than scared.

"Why would you shoot dad?" she came back indignantly, "He hasn't harmed you!"

"I won't ma'am, ef he don't make trouble." With that, Harrigan eased into the seat between them and gave further attention to the driver. He saw a man in the fifties, with furrowed, unsmiling features and stem lips. A face hard to read. His beard was neatly trimmed and the hands that grasped the lines were gnarled and capable. He sat still as an image, unmoved and taciturn. Beneath his dark coat, Hap saw a gun-belt buckled around his waist. Then the fugitive eyed the guards, now two wagons ahead and he fought another wave of panic. "Slide over a mite and give me the lines," he directed.

Without haste, the driver turned and weighed him with cold eyes. "One yip and them guards would come arunnin'," he said unemotionally.

"One yip," came back Harrigan harshly, "and you're buzzard bait — I kin only die once."

Impatience brittled his voice as he jammed the gun harder into the bearded man's ribs, "Git over — and gimme the lines!"

Not a muscle in the driver's furrowed features moved and he made no attempt to comply.

"This is it!" thought the fugitive and his eyes sought the river. Better that than the Snake Pen. He thumbed back the hammer of the .45.

At sound of the hammer click, the girl's voice, tight with urgency, broke the tension, "Humor him, dad! Please! Don't you see he's desperate? He's a killer."

With a grunt, her father slid along the seat.

A great relief flooded the fugitive. He reached over with his left hand and took the lines. Lowering the hammer of the .45, he stuck it beneath his waistband, hooking a thumb in the belt above it. "You show good sense, mister," he drawled, "What's your handle?"

"Findley," supplied the girl.

"Wal, Findley, I gotta cross the river. I'm Tom Findley, your son, if them wolves fire any questions. Act sensible and no one will be hurt. Buck — and you git it!"

He shook the team into motion as the wagon ahead pulled onto the quay. Slowly they eased down the slope of the river bank, the wheels dragging as they sank deep into the sand.

Blinding, the sun slid above the horizon, burnishing the river with flashing gold, and gave Harrigan good excuse to yank his Stetson low, covering his blond hair and shading his smashed nose.

The quay was clear. He drew a deep breath and clucked to the mules. Hooves drummed on wood and the wagon rolled across the platform.

Scatterguns in their hands and revolvers buckled around their middles, the three guards advanced. One circled to the rear of the wagon; the others came up on either side. From beneath the brim of his Stetson Harrigan eyed the man-hunters and uttered a silent prayer that his features were as unfamiliar to them as theirs were to him.

He stole a glance at the girl. Fingers interlocked, she stared at the fort across the river, its flag stirred sluggishly by vagrant puffs of sage-scented air. Findley's features were unreadable.

The fugitive's right hand inched a little closer to the butt of the gun that pressed against his belly.

CHAPTER THREE

"PRISON BREAK, FOLKS," explained the nearest guard, a long-geared, bony-faced man. "Gotta search your wagon." His voice dragged and dark stubble prickled his jaw. Harrigan saw that his eyes were heavy as he squinted up at the three on the wagon seat.

"A break!" echoed the fugitive, with eager interest, "Many bust out?"

"Jest two," threw in the other guard, "Big feller and a younger rooster with blond hair. Dangerous as mad dogs! You wouldn't have lamped the jaspers, in guards' uniforms?"

Harrigan shook his head. "Nope, paw and me, we're jest driving through. Maybe the lobos hit for the river?"

"Mebbe!" agreed the bony-faced guard, with no interest. He'd been bombarded with theories ever since the alarm bell routed him out of bed and he had rushed down to the ferry slip the night before.

The fugitive's strumming nerves relaxed a trifle. There had been no recognition in the guard's tired eyes.

Behind the canvas, he could hear the remaining guard fumbling around as he searched the wagon.

The vehicle jerked as the searcher jumped down over the endgate, and the bony-faced guard motioned them to pull ahead.

Relief flooded Harrigan as he shook up the mules. The wagon rolled across the quay. He touched the team with the whip as the leaders balked at the swaying ferry. "You showed good sense, folks," he said softly, but he kept his right hand close to the gun.

Eight wagons — five unwieldy Merivale freighters and three Conestogas — ground across the sand flats on the further side of the river, heading into the desert. Harrigan passed the lines back to the sober-faced Findley and rolled a smoke. His tight-strung nerves relaxed and the dry desert air went to his head like wine.

The girl spoke and there was no mistaking the distaste in her voice, "May we say good-bye — and good riddance?"

Harrigan grinned and drew slowly upon his cigarette, figuring his next move. "You ain't herding me much longer, mister, gun or no gun," put in her father, frowning at the dust-powdered backs of the plodding team. "You git!"

"Where you heading for?" countered the fugitive.

"Tucson."

Two-thirds of the way back to Vulture Valley, reflected the other, but he couldn't hold them under his gun day and night through the long, toilsome trip. They could easily denounce him the first time the wagon circled to make camp, and what kind of a show would he have against a bunch of tough bullwhackers? But it was sure death, or recapture, to be set afoot within sight of the penitentiary, set high above the river behind him.

He eyed the girl. "Give me to sunup and I swear I'll pull out. Is that a deal?"

"Are we in a position to bargain?" Irritation iced her tones.

Harrigan shrugged. When the train made camp at sundown, he thought, he'd circulate around. Maybe he could find a job with one of the freight wagons. If not, he'd have to cut loose. He couldn't blame the Findleys for wanting to be rid of him. No one craved the company of an escaped convict.

With an annoyed frown, the girl appealed to her father, "Do we have to ride with this — killer — all day?"

"Mebbe!" he returned, noncommittally.

"Well, I'll ride inside the wagon!" She commenced to clamber across the seat, disdaining Harrigan's proffered assistance.

"No shenanigans, ma'am," he warned, tapping his gunbutt.

She sniffed and disappeared behind the canvas.

Throughout the morning the wagons crawled like a giant caterpillar, and seemingly no faster, across a great dun plain, scarred with broken rock, patched with squat mesquite and drab greasewood.

Silent hostility sparked between the two men on the wagon seat, and little talk was exchanged. Once Hap inquired, "What's your business?"

"Sheepman," came back Findley laconically.

"Ugh!" shuddered the fugitive and spoke no more. It was just his luck, he considered wryly, to be eased out of a tight by a lousy sheepherder.

While Findley gazed blankly ahead and the plodding team slowly ate up the miles, speculation seethed in the fugitive's mind. Did Slick Sam make it, or was he back in Yuma, shackled in the Snake Pen? Was Cheyenne Dan dead? He wanted the gambler alive, had thrown the slug at his shoulder, but his fingers were stiff and he was unused to the gun. If dead, Cheyenne's lips were sealed. As long as he remained alive, confession of his perjured testimony might some day be dragged out of him. That shooting was another charge. If ever he was dragged back to Yuma, he'd sure never come out again.

As the day wore on, teams wearied in the furnace heat and the wagons drifted apart. A rider came back at a gallop. Harrigan envied him the sturdy gelding he forked.

"Close up!" he yelled, "This is Apache country."

Unexpectedly, Joan Findley's voice sounded behind Harrigan, "I thought the Apaches were under control. Aren't there military garrisons stationed throughout Arizona?"

"Wal, ma'am," he replied dryly, "you might say wolves are under control, too, but they pull down plenty calves. This is Mesalero range and I've heard tell them red devils are more dangerous than diamondbacks, most as bad as the Chiricahuas."

With sundown they camped beneath drooping cottonwoods close by a stream that writhed out of a range of forlorn hills. Below high cutbanks, it had shrunk into a succession of muddied pools, warm and unsavory. But it was water, and conserved the precious supply in barrels roped to the wagons.

Red Rufe, a burly, swaggering fellow in a bright red shirt, was wagon boss of the Merivales. Harrigan guessed that the Findleys had disclosed his identity, which meant he'd have to cut loose at sunup. The calculating look in the wagon boss' eyes when he sauntered over to the Findleys' campfire and the quick, covert glances the bullwhackers threw in his direction were plain giveaways. Not that it mattered a damn, he told himself. No wagon boss would hold up his train two days while he returned a prisoner to Yuma — and earned fifty dollars!

After nightfall, Rufe had the teams driven inside the circle of wagons and posted sentries. Harrigan drew the graveyard shift. At midnight he was stirred into wakefulness by a booted foot and crawled out from beneath the canvas tarp Joan Findley had dropped beside him as he sat alone beside the dying campfire.

Heavy-eyed, he pulled on the heavy prison ankle-boots, sole remaining link with Yuma and strode outside the circle of wagons. Stars burned bright in silent splendor overhead and a wolf howled mournfully back in the hills. Recollection flowed into his mind of burnt wagons, bodies hacked beyond recognition, the frozen ghastliness that were the death masks of tortured men. A wagon train was a rich prize and there was scarce a week but that some marauding band of Apaches was not sacking and slaying upon a lonely trail.

The fugitive fell to considering his own lot and found scant pleasure in the prospect. Inquiry that evening had revealed no chance of a job. Rufe hitched up his gunbelt and declared emphatically there were no holes in the freighting outfit. The remaining two wagons were owned by nester families with no money and little chuck to feed an extra mouth. Now that word was around camp that he was a fugitive killer, odds were he would be run off at sunup. And what chance for a man afoot in the desert?

Way up the bed of the shrunken stream the hoot of a night owl, faint in the distance, floated to his ears. Another answered, close in. Harrigan tensed, listening with speculative eyes, his own troubles forgotten. He moved around the wagons until he came to another sentry, a whiskered bullwhacker, lolling against a wheel.

"What d'ye make of the owls?" he queried.

The bullwhacker spat. "What would I make of 'em? They ain't uncommon, but I'm danged ef I ever heard one at this camp spot afore."

Harrigan drifted back to his post. He thought of another such night, and a sleeping emigrant train he had hired out to lead through rugged Apache Pass, across endless miles of mesquite to the Chirihahua country, through the Dragoons and over the arid plains to Tucson. That other night the owls had hooted — death swooped with the dawn.

Around two, when his relief took over, he headed for the freighters' dead fire. Sleeping forms of the bullwhackers, a gun within reach of each, bulged around. He located the wagon boss, bent and touched his shoulder. Rufe was awake on the instant.

"There's Apache sign," said Harrigan tersely.

The big man eyed him with visible suspicion. "You plumb certain?" he asked doubtfully.

"Wal, I ain't partial to hoot owl signals."

Rufe threw off his soogans and reached quickly for his boots.

"There's no cause to get choused up," drawled Harrigan. "The rattlesnakes most never attack before sunup."

"Mebbeso, but I'll double the guard and rouse camp," declared the wagon boss.

"You sure don't take no chances!" There was a touch of derision in the fugitive's voice. He could not forget that he'd have to face the desert, alone, in a few hours.

"Thet's why I still got my hair," grunted the other. "Reckon we'll hobble the mules, they'll panic ef there's trouble."

Nursing a borrowed Winchester, Harrigan lay beneath the wagon and watched a luminous haze above the horizon that heralded dawn. Faintly discernible in the grayness, Findley was sprawled beside him, a Sharps 50.70 held loosely to his shoulder. In the wagon, between two spooled rolls, the sheepman had placed his daughter, despite her protests.

Around the circle other men crouched behind wagons or stared out into the dimness between the spokes of wheels, tensed in the chill of a desert dawn.

Light grew stronger in the east and the stars dimmed overhead, but there was still no sign of the dreaded Apaches. Harrigan wondered if his nerves had made a jackass out of him. He visioned the wagon boss' disgust and the bullwhackers' profanity over their broken night's rest.

A breeze soughed across the flats, rustling softly through the tinder-dry brush. Then the air was alive with a louder rustling — the flight of feathered arrows. Almost instantly, the brooding quiet was shattered by the wobbling shrieks of attacking Apaches. Naked except for turbans and breech-cloths, braves rose like painted specters out of the brush and leapt in for the kill.

The Apache stakes all upon the shock of a surprise attack — and this was no surprise. The deep boom of Sharps mingled with the brisk ping of Winchester repeaters as the yelling braves rushed frenziedly for the wagons. Brown bodies were cut down by the whining lead, but more shrieking savages swarmed in.

From beneath the Findley wagon, Harrigan levered and fired, levered and fired, picking out darting, naked figures against the lightening skyline. One savage in dirty breech-cloth reached the wagon, jumped upon the wheel and hacked through the canvas before a heavy slug from the sheepman's Sharps knocked him down. Harrigan, swinging his barrel, took another racing madly past the end-gate. It was impossible to judge in the bedlam of shrieking savages, cursing men, braying mules and incessant gunfire whether the Apaches had broken through the wagon line or not. Harrigan could only loose lead at every turbaned figure that bobbed into sight and hope fervently that no savage would sneak in from behind and split his skull.

Then he became conscious that the shrieking attackers had disappeared as completely and mysteriously as the dying night. Triumphant shouting arose from the wagons. Arrows began to swish in again, silent and deadly.

Findley grunted queerly. Harrigan's head slewed around, to see the sheepman's left hand locked upon the feathered haft of an arrow protruding from his shoulder, agony written upon his bearded features.

Harrigan jumped to his feet, grabbed the stricken man beneath the arms and dragged him towards the rear of the wagon. He parted the canvas, "Miss Findley! Quick, ma'am!"

A stubby .32 tight-gripped in her right fist, the girl peered out. Her face blanched as she glimpsed her father's prostrate form and the feathered shaft. A sudden shriek from the girl brought Harrigan's head around ... to stare almost into the distorted features of a brave who, blood streaming from a head wound, had risen from the ground. Tomahawk whistling, the Apache hurled at him. He twisted, instinctively raised an arm that he knew would be powerless to ward off the blow. A shot whipcracked. The Apache's mouth slackened, the tomahawk slipped out of his nerveless hand and flew over Harrigan's head. Dead upon his feet, the brave crashed into the end-gate and his lifeless form fell almost at the fugitive's feet.

Breathing hard, Harrigan eyed the bronze body and then stared around in search of the marksman. A gasp of horror brought his glance up to the wagon. Joan Findley was standing, ashen-faced, staring, first at the smoking gun in her hand, then at the slack form of the dead Apache.

"B'gosh, ma'am, you're fast!" he ejaculated. "Give me a hand with your paw!"

Hands trembling, she put the gun away and climbed down. Between them, they boosted the sheepman into the wagon.

The din had died now and Harrigan surmised that the Apaches had pulled off. The surprise attack had been smashed, and the Apache seldom stomached a daylight fight.

Joan Findley spread a bedroll and Harrigan laid her father upon it. With his Barlow knife, he cut away the wounded man's shirt. Joan knelt beside him. The arrow had transfixed Findley's right shoulder. Its sharp, flint head emerged through the muscles below the arm.

"Go get another man!" directed Harrigan sharply.

"I can help!" she protested, lips white.

"Not with this job — you stay outside."

Without another word, she dropped down over the end-gate. When she returned with Rufe, who was in roaring good humor, Harrigan had whittled off the feathered haft.

"You hold him," he told the big wagon boss, "and I'll yank."

"Wait!" cried the girl. She quickly tore up a clean towel.

Harrigan rolled the sheepman upon his face and gripped the arrowhead. Rufe set two heavy hands upon the wounded man's shoulders. Joan turned away.

A gasp of agony — and the job was done.

The girl swiftly plugged the gaping wounds.

"There," said the wagon boss, picking up the Barlow knife and hacking a chaw off a plug of tobacco, "is a gal with guts. Me, I like 'em that way."

A tally revealed that there were two men killed, two so badly slashed that they had to be packed in a wagon, and three slightly wounded. No one took time to count the dead Apaches lying around.

The dead men were buried in soft earth beside the river. Black buzzards, already circling low, would take care of the Indians.

To the bullwhackers, the attack was an incident, a risk of their trade. Death was always close upon the desert.

Harrigan had no need to worry about employment now. Rufe gave him credit for saving the camp and handed him a bull-whacker's whip. But the fugitive returned it, "I got a job," he said.

Camp broke up for a late start. Harrigan harnessed the Findley mules and climbed onto the wagon seat. "All ready to go, ma'am?" he inquired, pushing aside the canvas.

Joan rose from beside her father's still form. "Drive care-fully!" she entreated.

"It's a rough ride, ma'am, no matter how you take it," he said, with a wry quirk of the lips, "How's your paw doing?" He had acquired a dead man's razor and his stubbled beard was gone. With it he seemed to have scraped a dozen years off his age.

"I hope he'll be all right," she assured him dubiously, "but I'm afraid of infection." She regarded Harrigan's shaven features curiously, "You don't look like a — a killer!"

"From one killer to another, ma'am," he grinned, "I ain't thet kind of a killer. Git up, mules!" Harrigan was in high spirits.

After the Apache attack, Joan Findley's hostility to the fugi-tive evaporated. By day, she spent most of her time beside her father, but Harrigan lived for the evenings, when the plains slowly purpled and the tang of burning mesquite mingled with the pungent scent of the sage. Then Joan would sit opposite him at the fire and they would talk. He learned that she had taught school, but had quit to keep house when her mother died. Her father had run sheep in Montana, but had sold out and migrated to Arizona, attracted by stories of limitless range. Her three elder brothers had gone ahead and were already in Tucson.

Close connection with sheep was the only flaw in what the fugitive regarded as Joan Findley's perfection. Like every cattleman and puncher, he had no use for "stinkers" and less for "snoozers" or sheepmen. But then, he considered, no girl could have everything.

"Why did they confine you in that horrible penitentiary?" she asked one evening. Her candid eyes met his, "I know you too well now, Hap, to believe you could commit murder."

He fumbled for his cigarette papers and gazed gloomily into the spitting flames of the dry mesquite. The question awakened poignant memories, memories that arose like ghosts out of the past. He lit his cigarette with a twig from the fire and drew upon it somberly, "It's a long story, ma'am. Maybe it's best not told."

"But I want to hear it," she insisted.

"Wal, I own 640 acres east of Buzzard Gap — thet's in Vulture Valley, Apache County — Bubbling Spring they call it. I got the best water in Arizona. Bull Flint rods the Turtle to the south. Thet's a big spread. The Arizona Cattle Company, a Limey outfit, runs the ACC to the north. Flint craved my water, bad. Offered to buy me out, but I wouldn't sell. Tried to drive me out, but me and Harry, my pard, we stuck. Next he swears we sleepered his calves, which was a damned lie. Horrman, the banker in town, he fancied the spread, too. Made me likely offers, but I warn't selling." He rose, threw another armful of brush on the fire. Joan waited patiently, fingers interlocked, nursing her knees. Harrigan hunkered again, "Harry's uncle rodded the Circle H, east side of the valley. He died a year or so back and left no will, so his dinero was tied up in the Valley Bank. Wal, the court finally awarded it to Harry. We rode to town and he drew it out, $20,000. Said he always craved to find out how it felt to pack around real money. We gravitate to The Double Eagle and licker up some. Harry drifts away and I reel around the saloon like a pup trying to find a spot to lay down."

Joan smiled and he grinned back, a trifle shame-faced. "I ain't excusing myself. I was tucked away in a corner, drowsing, when Limpy Leeman, the deputy, hotfoots into the saloon and gathers me in — with a little assistance. Next morning I wakes up in a cell with a taste in my mouth like I'd had supper with a coyote and I learns the charge is murder. Harry was found in the alley next to the saloon, with a bullet through his back. Cheyenne Dan, a gambler, swore he saw me plug Harry, grab his dinero and ditch the gun. And Chunky Nabor, Flint's foreman, backs Cheyenne's hand. They claim I musta cached the greenbacks." Harrigan spat his half-smoked cigarette into the fire. "The lousy sidewinders! I stood trial. Judge deals out twelve years, said I'd have swung ef I hadn't been drinking. Wal, thet's how I come to be corralled in Yuma."

Joan Findley followed his story with furrowed brow. "You — you didn't shoot Harry and were too drunk to remember?" she ventured.

Harrigan laughed shortly. "Me shoot Harry, the best pard I ever had! You're loco, ma'am! Heck, ef I felt thataway I coulda plugged him out on the range and no one would have been the wiser. Nope, Bull Flint framed me to get Bubbling Spring. Cheyenne's evidence was bought, Chunky sided his boss and Limp Leeman's crooked — they split the dinero. Thet's how I size the hand up."

"Why did you shoot the gambler in Yuma?"

"Cheyenne Dan!"

"And what will you do now — if you escape recapture?" she inquired gently.

"Head for Vulture Valley."

"But they'll arrest you again!"

"Maybe I kin handle that," he returned stubbornly.

"Don't be foolish, Hap!" Impulsively, Joan reached out and grasped his forearm, and he thrilled to her touch. "Fate has been unkind to you, but don't seek revenge. Can't you see you haven't a chance? If you kill this Bull Flint or Chunky or Leeman, you'll be caught, sooner or later, and you'll be hung. Ride north — Montana's a grand state, or cross the Border. Start again!"

"And leave Bubbling Spring f'r them buzzards! No ma'am!"

CHAPTER FOUR

THE SETTING SUN bathed the ragged peaks of the Dragoons with blood when a buckskin, hock-scarred and gaunt from long travel, jogged into the cowtown known as Powwow. Straddling the double-cinched Texas saddle was a loose-jointed young rider with a belligerent jaw. Cropped, curly hair showed raven black beneath a stained Stetson and the bristles of a black mustache, stiff as a scrub brush, prickled his upper lip.

When Limpy had hustled him into the stage to stand trial at Apache City, reflected Harrigan, he was a sorrel-top, clean-shaven, with a straight nose. The crooked nose with which they'd presented him in Yuma, plus dye and the newly acquired mustache, should prove sufficient disguise, particularly since no one would figure he'd be loco enough to head back to Vulture Valley. It was doubtful, too, if word of his escape had sifted through yet, with the county seat forty miles distant.

Powwow hadn't changed a mite, he decided, as the ruts that marked the wagon road stretched out to become a wide sandy street, hock-deep in powdery dust. The same high square-fronted buildings, gray and weathered, slumbered behind the creaky plankwalks — McArdle's Store, with sacks piled on its gallery; the U. S. Barber Shop; Jigg's Hash House; Buskin's Saddle Shop. The rock-and-adobe Valley Bank frowned on the corner. Bill Moggs' dilapidated livery barn, with its sagging roof, still appeared on the verge of collapse, as it had for the past ten years.

At sight of the deputy sheriff's law shack, the rider's hand tightened on the reins — damn that crooked lawman!

From the Mexican quarter, across Gunsmoke Creek, willow-fringed to his left, floated the tin tinkle of a guitar, oddly plaintive in the still evening air.

No, nothing had changed, the alert-eyed Harrigan decided. Then he remembered, he hadn't been gone more than four months. It seemed a lifetime.

No signs of life were apparent except in the vicinity of The Double Eagle, where a row of drowsing ponies were tied to the rail and the drone of voices rolled over the batwings.

Pulse quickening, Harrigan kneed the buckskin and pulled in to the water trough beside the saloon. This was the showdown, he considered, as the weary animal sucked thirstily. Baldy the barkeep, and most of the habituees of the saloon, knew him. If his disguise bluffed them he was sitting pretty in Vulture Valley.

He loose-knotted the buckskin's reins around the gnawed hitchrail, ducked beneath it and, with speeding pulse, headed for the doorway.

As the batwings squealed inward, Harrigan's glance flicked around — over the sprinkling of men bellied up to the wooden bar that ran parallel to the left side of the long, low-ceilinged room; the intent groups of card players bunched around the worn baize of card tables; the women with carmined lips slow-circling in the arms of trail-stained punchers in a cleared space at the back, while a blonde, with plump, silken legs, strummed a waltz upon a weary piano.

The fugitive's pulse eased a little when he failed to focus on Deputy Sheriff Limpy Leeman's gaunt features. Limpy's bitter eyes were like an eagle's. He could read a blotched brand quicker than any man in the Valley.

With growing confidence, Harrigan jingled across the sandy floor, stepped up to the bar and beat the dust from his Stetson against his pant leg. Baldy, the fleshy barkeep, wheezed towards him, "What'll it be, mister?" he squeaked in his shrill treble, wiping off the smooth bar top from force of habit.

"Slug of bourbon!"

Baldy glanced at his face incuriously, set a bottle and glass before him and waddled away. Harrigan breathed deep, he was over the first hurdle. He poured a short drink and sipped it leisurely.

Again his nerves tightened as he glimpsed Chunky Nabor, Bull Flint's foreman, ferret eyes sunk deep in chubby features, seated amid a bunch of Turtle riders at a card table. Close by, a red-headed rider yawned over a bottle of beer. Devilment was stamped upon his freckled features and he wore his gun thonged down. Droop-Eye, the booze-soaked swamper, slunk around the card tables like a stray mongrel nosing for tidbits, eager to pick up the price of a drink.

Smoking a slender cheroot as always, Whitey Wakeman, who ran the joint, was dealing in a high-stake game with two cowmen and the storekeeper. Whitey, mused the fugitive, was as slick as the grease on his smoothly brushed hair. He had the pale, chiselled features and carefully manicured hands of the professional gambler, but his eyes were slippery. The bulge of a hide-away was plain beneath his tight-fitting black coat.

The piano player quit and the dancers headed for the bar. Around Harrigan, the air became heavy with scent as the painted ladies and their partners crowded close. With distaste, he dropped a silver coin beside his bottle and headed for a vacant table.

Rolling a smoke, the fugitive stretched luxuriously to ease his saddle-cramped limbs. He was back in Powwow — now what?

"Aren't you going to buy me a drink, dearie?"

Harrigan's head jerked up. The piano-playing blonde had plunked into the seat beside him. She was plump but still shapely, and it was plain she was not a blonde. A heavy mop of yellow hair, obviously bleached, was heaped high upon her head and secured with combs that glittered with paste jewels. Bracelets tinkled upon her bare arms and a green silk dress, cut too short, top and bottom, clung to her curves like a second skin. The scarlet upon her lips made vivid contrast with the pale cream of her rounded features. There was a curious seductiveness in her husky tones and allure lurked around her full lips. Harrigan had met dance hall floozies before, but this girl — new to The Double Eagle — possessed a robustness, a forthrightness, that puzzled him.

"Say, mister!" Her dark eyes flashed, "You're not buying me — just a drink — I hope!"

"Sure!" he agreed shortly, and pitched a gold eagle on the table top.

Curiously, he watched as she threaded nonchalantly between the tables, carelessly repelling an amorous puncher with a hard push from a robust arm.

She returned and set out bottle and glasses.

"A man of your quality wouldn't be needing the change?" There was subtle mockery in her voice as she dropped down again beside him.

"Keep it!" he said carelessly, "if you need it more than I do."

"You can always tell your ma you spent it on a wild woman," she suggested mischievously, her dark eyes appraising him.

Harrigan grunted and they eyed each other squarely. He was trying to figure out what there was about this make-believe blonde that attracted him.

"Ain't you drinking?" He nodded at the bottle.

"Had mine at the bar."

"Like hell you did! You wanted a percentage on the sale."

"Right, wise guy!" White teeth flashed as her lips curved with amusement. "Maybe I can bring another bottle?"

"Your price is too steep."

"You forget the companionship!" Again, her flashing eyes mocked him. She took in his dusty garb. "You riding through — or staying awhile?"

Harrigan's eyes sought the stairway against the rear wall that led to gambling rooms and cubicles on the second floor, "Not with you, sister!" he came back curtly.

"Say, did I ask for that crack?" The blonde's voice thickened with anger and fire smouldered in her eyes. "You cheap —! Do you think any girl can be bought for a lousy dollar?"

"I guess they can around here!" he retorted with growing resentment.

Like an unleashed spring, she sprang to her feet. There was a silvery tinkle of bracelets as her hand reached out and fastened upon his wrist. He marvelled at the strength of her grip as she almost hauled him off the chair.

"Come on, smarty pants, I want to show you something!" she snapped.

Harrigan rose. It was either that or create a scene, and this was no time to draw undue attention to himself.

Hauling him as though he was a rebellious boy, the blonde strode towards the front window of the saloon. There she jabbed a forefinger against the fly-specked glass. Across the street was a vacant lot, and on one side sat the saddler's square store. Behind it, standing alone, was a small clapboard shack, indistinct in the starlight.

"See that shack!" The throaty voice was tight. "That's mine! I work here, I sleep there — alone! And if you, or any other desert canary, strays around, I'm always ready to welcome you — with a shotgun!"

"Hey, Ruby!" shrilled a girl perched on the bar, "Give us some more music!" Other voices joined in the demand. Breast heaving beneath her low-cut dress, the blonde flounced away.

Harrigan remained by the window, uncomfortably aware from the grins upon the studiously averted faces of nearby card players that the scene had been played to an attentive audience. The piano started thumping again, thumping with a viciousness that threatened to snap the sagging wires.

"Perk up, pard!" He turned to meet the amused glance of the red-headed rider, still nursing his warm beer. "You roped the wrong heifer. Build another loop — you can't miss!"

Bottling his irritation, Harrigan grinned and headed for the bar again. Stretching out another drink, he set a foot on the rail and fell to considering his future actions. Since parting from the Findleys at Tucson he had pushed his pony to the limit to reach Powwow. Now that he had arrived, he felt suddenly at a loss. If he was not to remain a fugitive as long as he lived, or was recaptured, he had to clear his name, which meant uncovering Harry's killer, and proving the murderer's guilt. Three men could supply the evidence — Cheyenne Dan, in Yuma, maybe dead; Chunky Nabor, the Turtle foreman, who hated his guts, and Limpy Leeman, the deputy sheriff. Chunky had Bull Flint and the big Turtle outfit to back his hand; Limpy was as cagey as a gray wolf, and as dangerous.

Deep in thought, the fugitive stared into the back-bar mirror. His eyes narrowed and tension again clamped down. A tall, gaunt man was pushing through the batwings. A metal star was pinned to his loose-hanging vest and a heavy Colt was holstered around his hips. He paused inside the door, his eyes, deep-set in bony features, probing around in harsh, unblinking gaze. A tobacco-stained mustache straggled over a thin-lipped mouth that drooped at the corners, producing an effect of brooding bitterness. Like a black buzzard, considered the tensed Harrigan, and with about as much heart.

His cold scrutiny completed, Leeman limped towards the bar, extending no greetings and receiving none. A bullet from the gun of a long-forgotten bandit had smashed the kneecap and stiffened his left leg. Three years previously, a small-pox epidemic had swept away his wife and two small children. Maybe he had cause to be bitter.

The lawman crooked an elbow beside Harrigan. Their glances met and locked in the back-bar mirror. Baldy set a bottle and glass before the newcomer and waddled away.

The lawman poured slowly, his eyes reluctant to leave Harrigan's reflection in the mirror. His head half-turned, "Riding through, mister?"

Harrigan's hackles rose at the sound of his voice, as uncompromising as his features. "Maybe!"

Limpy tossed down his drink, the furrows across his forehead deepening. He sat down the empty glass and imperceptibly eased closer. Harrigan poured carefully a full glass.

"Ain't we met afore — somewheres?" persisted the deputy.

The fugitive's fingers tightened upon the glass, half raised to his lips. "I reckon not!" He tried to make it seem offhand.

But the lawman was not satisfied. His expressionless eyes fastened upon the other's features, analyzing, weighing, pondering. He came to a decision, "Guess you best step down tuh the office with me, feller!"

"Sure!" agreed Harrigan softly. His right wrist flipped. He flung the contents of his glass full into the deputy's gaunt face. Blinded by the stinging liquor, Limpy jerked erect, tears streaming from his tortured eyes and whisky dripping off his chin. He stabbed for his gun. But Harrigan sidestepped. His bunched fist sank into the lawman's middle with a vicious jab. Limpy doubled like a closed jackknife, grunting with pain. The fugitive slammed him against the bar with a swinging left beside the jaw, whipped out his own gun and backed rapidly towards the batwings.

It was all over in a few savage seconds. No one around was apparently aware of the byplay. The card players still slapped down their pasteboards and the shrill laughter of the girls mingled with the shuffle of dancing feet as the blonde murdered the *Blue Danube*.

Leeman grabbed the edge of the bar and hauled himself erect. His gun came out and he loosed a slug — blind.

All sound ceased at the thunder of the Colt. Every eye was focused upon the reeling deputy, smoking gun held impotently in his right fist while he scrubbed at his streaming eyes with his bandanna. Then they glimpsed Harrigan's silent form, half-crouched as he back-tracked towards the street.

"Git thet jasper!" yelled the blinded deputy.

But no one moved. The saloon was hushed, save for the shuffle of the fugitive's boots.

The blonde at the piano suddenly screamed. Out of his field of vision at the card tables, the flat ugly crack of metal upon a skull came to the fugitive's ears. He swivelled upon the balls of his feet, gun levelled. Chunky Nabor, a six-gun sliding out of his nerveless fingers, was slipping sideways out of his chair. Behind him, the red-headed puncher, features bleak, covered the surprised Turtle riders.

Harrigan was close to the street now. He pushed out, stood beneath the plankwalk canopy and eyed the interior of the saloon across the batwings. The deputy was still dabbing at his smarting eyes, the girls had fluttered together like flurried hens, Red was swiftly backing out in his wake.

The redhead hurricaned through the batwings and almost bowled the watching Harrigan over.

"I'm thanking you, Red!" ejaculated the fugitive, steadying.

The other chuckled and holstered his gun, "Where you headin' for?"

"Hell-and-gone, I guess."

"I know a likelier spot — tail me!"

With that the redhead stepped quickly to the rail and loosed a pony. Harrigan untied the buckskin and swung into leather. Red was already spurring down street. Harrigan gave his mount the steel and pounded in pursuit. The yellow light that patched the ground from the square windows of The Double Eagle dropped behind. He finally pulled up to the stirrup of Red's galloping pony. Together, they hurtled into the friendly darkness.

CHAPTER FIVE

THE LAST of the shacks that fringed Powwow faded into the night behind them and the yellow ruts of the wagon road snaked southward across the swales ahead. Shadows patched the brushy flat. The night was still save for the rhythmic thud of the ponies' hooves upon the sun-baked ground.

Red pulled his hard-breathing pony down to a trot, checked it, head half turned. Taut in the saddle beside him, Harrigan heard a distant shout, the faint drum of many hooves.

"Limpy's loosed his dawgs," drawled the redhead with no concern, "I gamble there ain't a jasper on the posse who could track a wagon through a boghole." With that, he angled off through the brush, walking his pony in a wide half-circle back in the direction of town.

The tattoo of hooves upon the hardened ground was plain now. The fugitives pulled rein in the shadow of a clump of manzanita. A few hundred paces distant, a string of riders thundered along the wagon road south.

"Lissen to thet bunch of stampedin' steers awhooping and ahollering," murmured Red. "I gamble they don't feel kindly towards Limpy f'r deputizing them. They love thet old tarantula like the devil loves Holy Water."

He heeled his pony as the sound of the posse's progress died southward and they hit back for Powwow. Skirting the sleeping town, Red held steadily northward. Harrigan asked no questions. It was plain his new-found pard knew where he was riding and he was curious to see just what the redhead was heading for.

It was plain that Red was puncher, the thonged-down holster was the badge of a gunman. It was plain, too, that he had no respect for the law. Now that Limpy was on his trail again, considered the fugitive wryly, he needed a hideaway.

For awhile Red followed the curves of Gunsmoke Creek, looping down from the foothills of the Dragoons. Then he cut away from the stream, angling westward across the flat plain. Ahead, mountains were dim-shadowed against the star-sprinkled sky. Occasional bunches of cows moved uneasily out of their path. It was too dark to read the brands.

Red broke a silence that had laid long between them, "I never could abide a sneak draw!"

"Which was why you conked Chunky!" Harrigan grinned at the recollection.

"How come you knew it was Chunky Nabor?" shot back the redhead, and his head swung around in curt inquiry. Harrigan inwardly cursed his too ready tongue.

"Heard a cowpoke give him the handle," he lied lamely. "Ain't he segundo of the Turtle?"

"Nope," threw back Red, reassured, "He done quit, tied up with the Limey outfit thet rods the ACC." His irrepressible chuckle reached Hap's ears, "You oughta lamp the boss — a Limejuicer who rides a saddle like a mustard plaster and sticks a winder in his eye. A hundred per cent gold-plated dood!"

Harrigan digested the information. He knew the Arizona Cattle Company, a spread even larger than Bull Flint's Turtle, that ranged the upper part of Vulture Valley with Gunsmoke Creek dividing the two outfits. His peanut spread at Bubbling Spring was sandwiched between the two and both craved to lay hands on it. If it wasn't for Bubbling Spring, he considered somberly, Harry wouldn't lie in boothill and he wouldn't be a fugitive.

Gradually, as they jogged towards the mountains, the terrain heaved up into rolling hills, smooth-topped and seamed with cow paths. Harrigan followed his companion's lead, disguising the fact that he knew this country better than the palm of his hand. He could see now that the redhead was heading for Buzzard Gap, for twenty miles, the only break in the sprawling chain of mountains that were the Dragoons. And below the Gap lay Bubbling Spring. He opened his mouth to fire a question, closed it abruptly. His tongue had almost tripped him already.

They rode across a bouldery bench. Below, where the terrain flattened to form a small, saucerlike valley, lay his spread. He strained his eyes, itching to glimpse it again, thought he could discern the outline of the little adobe ranch house he once called home.

"Say, ain't that a spread down yonder?" he ejaculated, unable to hold himself longer.

"Yep," drawled Red carelessly, "A two-bit outfit, but good water. Two pards rodded it, they claim. One bored the other and drew twelve years. Reckon he's plaiting hair bridles in Yuma. Ain't no one around now."

Chests heaving, the ponies dropped to a walk, ironshod hooves striking sparks from the rock-bound trail that snaked up to the Gap. Grotesque in the wan light, eroding pinnacles rose around them and the sobbing, half-human shriek of a mountain lion echoed and died amid the crags.

The mountain walls closed in and the two rode into the gloom of the pass. Powdery talus dust rose in a choking fog and the sky above was a ragged ribbon between the beetling cliffs.

For a mile or more, the ponies plodded like gray ghosts along the rock-littered pass, then the walls dropped abruptly away and the canopy of the heavens again spread overhead.

Tailing Red, who was working north through a tangle of canyons, Harrigan knew that Alkali Valley lay to his left and that they were heading into the malpais, long a rendezvous of renegades and rustlers.

Wearied by long hours in the saddle, he was nodding when his companion swung off into a narrow draw. They pushed through a stand of scrub oak and the red glow of a campfire punched through the darkness ahead.

Harrigan, fully awake now, glimpsed six or more hard-faced hombres hunkered around the dancing flames. Behind them, the face of the cliff was split asunder and the gap yawned black, forming a vast cave. Ponies were picketted in the brush.

With a cheerful hail, Red swung out of the saddle and approached the fire, Harrigan behind him. Expressionless eyes focussed the newcomer in silent scrutiny.

A battered old renegade rose and shuffled forward. His features were seamed like weathered rawhide and the left side of his mouth was puckered into an eternal snarl by an old bullet scar. When he spoke, his voice was soft — like the purr of a panther. "How come you brung a stranger into camp, Red?"

Nowise flurried, the redhead grinned cheerfully, "Now don't start aclimbing my hump, Colorado, this jasper's on the lam." Hoarse chuckles ran around the fire as he recounted the fracas in the Double Eagle and the tricking of the posse. Only Colorado stood frowning.

"And what's yore moniker, feller?" he demanded of Harrigan.

The fugitive thought fast. "Yuma," he came back.

"Ever handled stock?"

"Never knowed nothing else."

The renegade leader rasped his bristly jaw, pale eyes weighing the newcomer. "Yuma," he ruminated, half to himself, "Mebbe you know the Snake Pen?"

"Would I ever forget it?" said Harrigan, his voice grim with remembrance. He held out his wrists.

Colorado nodded, "Me, too," he said softly. Then he swung around to the riders at the fire. "Meet Yuma, boys — he's in!"

Beneath his soogans, Harrigan lay on his back and dreamily eyed the clustered stars. Close by, the fire guttered into embers and around him were lumped the forms of sleeping renegades.

Lady Luck sure played heck with a man's good intentions, he pondered. He had ridden back to Powwow determined to bring Harry's killer to justice and side the law. Within twelve hours he had assaulted the deputy sheriff, dodged a posse and joined a gang of renegades. Where would the trail lead next?

At sunup he was astir, but the men around him slept on. Higher up the draw he found a small spring trickling over mossy boulders. He washed and shaved, watered the buckskin. By that time, a rheumy-eyed oldster, with flabby jowls like a bloodhound, was stirring up the fire. Red's shock of fiery hair bobbed out from beneath his soogans. He grinned, yawned and began to yank on his boots. The redhead would grin, thought Harrigan, with a rope around his neck.

"These gents sleep late," he commented, dropping down beside Red.

"Heck," chuckled the other, "They work nights."

"Doing what?"

"Stick around, pard, you'll find out!"

Throughout that day the gang killed time, whiling away the hours with listless card games and frequent trips into the cave to sample the contents of two gallon crocks of raw liquor. When the sinking sun threw shadows across the draw, however, the gang stirred into brisk activity. Ponies were watered and saddled. The cook suspended a huge pot of coffee over the fire and Colorado cached the whisky crocks.

At nightfall, eight riders filed through the squat oaks. The moon rode high and serene when they fogged through the Gap and dropped down the benches into Vulture Valley.

Silent as the shadow of a cloud drifting across the swales, the block of riders headed north, boring into ACC range.

Harrigan had no illusions now, it was plain he was tied up to a gang of rustlers. Colorado, jogging ahead, led them towards a low range of hills, passing up the long files of cows that plodded slowly down to Gunsmoke Creek.

They rounded the shoulder of a ridge and Harrigan caught the reflection of moonlight upon water. As they drew closer he recognized the spot, Smooth Water. A spring, running down a narrow draw, had been dammed, forming a wide pond. Around it, cows were bunched like swarming bees.

Colorado led them past the reservoir, wheeled. The rustlers strung out as methodically as U.S. cavalrymen. Then, a long line of yelling men, they rode back, chousing the beef with rope and voice, combing the vicinity of the reservoir clean.

Harrigan, swallowing dust in the drag, marvelled at the simplicity and audacity of the plan. In the past there had been spasmodic rustling in the Valley. But never anything like this. There must be, he figured, three hundred prime steers in the bellowing herd rolling towards the Gap. And Colorado's gang was coolly hazing them off ACC range without sign of a night guard or slightest attempt at opposition. This was a rustlers' paradise. The Limey, thought Harrigan contemptuously, must be loco to let them get away with it. Granted the ACC herds ran into thousands, no outfit could survive leakage like this.

Red loomed out of the dust haze and reined beside him. "Wal, how d'ye fancy yore new job?" he sang out cheerily above the clacking of horns and rumble of hooves.

"I'd jest as soon herd milk cows," came back Harrigan. "There's a mite more excitement."

"Yep," agreed Red, "This drive is as easy as slutting a gut, but we trade lead occasional."

"Ain't the ACC wise?"

Red's irrepressible chuckle answered him.

It was a long-drawn-out, laborious task urging the protesting herd up the steep, winding trail to the Gap and trailing them through the gloomy recesses of the tortuous pass. With any kind of opposition reflected Harrigan, whose shirt stuck to his back and right arm ached from swinging a rope, it would have been impossible.

Dawn grayed the pinnacles and the rising sun struck fire from the naked peaks when the weary, sore-footed herd was choused through the narrow neck of a box canyon, deep in the malpais. A three-strand wire fence stretched across the canyon, behind which more rustled cows lumped in a dun mass.

Harrigan swore beneath his breath — this was big business.

Poles were set across the entrance and the rustlers, leaving the beef securely corralled, headed for their hideaway.

Queries prickled in Harrigan's mind. "How in hell d'ye cash in on the beef?" he demanded of Red. "The Border's a three-day drive and they could trail that bunch as easy as a herd of elephants."

"Being regular cowmen, with a registered brand, we ship it," returned the redhead with comic gravity.

"Not from Apache City, the county seat?"

"Nope, from Mesa. That's a way station of the Western Pacific sixty miles north through the mountains and one hell of a drive. Mesa ain't much more'n a telegraph office, loading pens and a water tank."

"Branded ACC!" Harrigan's voice was incredulous.

"Heck no, we gotta doctor them brands. When the cows reach the cars they're 000 Barred." Red traced ACC on his dusty saddle skirt, joined the ends of the C's, circled the A and drew a line through the whole. "Git it? It's a natural!"

Harrigan could not repress an answering grin. "You jaspers got more gall than brass monkeys, and Colorado's a brainy cuss."

"Heck," came back Red carelessly, "He don't do the figgerin'."

"Say, jest who does ramrod this outfit?"

Red built a smoke, lifted his shoulders. "Who gives a damn, as long as he pays out?"

Harrigan chewed on this new aspect of the gang with creased brow. Who was the kingpin? He thought of Chunky Nabor, Flint's foreman, switching to the ACC. Chunky knew better than to let the spread be rustled blind. Was the Turtle owner playing a crooked game, with Chunky as his tool — robbing his neighbor and fattening his bankroll? If he would have a man murdered to grab a spring he would be likely to do just that. Which meant that he — Harrigan — was doing Flint's dirty work and helping put dollars into his pocket. It didn't set right.

Camp was shifted to the canyon the following afternoon and the dusty, disagreeable job of botching the brands commenced. Two days later, Colorado and Harrigan rode back to the old hideaway, alone. The remainder of the gang were trailing the herd displaced by the last gather through the mountains to Mesa.

Daylight was dying when the pair rode in. Harrigan stripped the gear off the ponies while Colorado kindled a fire the tough old renegade was as sparing with words as a miser with dollars, and Harrigan had too much on his mind to attempt to make talk. They hunkered on opposite sides of the fire like wooden Indians, sucking their cigarettes and staring into the flames.

The longer Harrigan mulled over the situation, the less he liked it. Cattle rustling went against his grain, and rustling for the benefit of the man he believed had framed him for a killing soured him right through.

Colorado's cigarette butt made a fiery arc as he tossed it aside, rose and moved towards the ponies. Harrigan watched his squat form disappear into the darkness, heard him saddling up, then a steady clip-clop as he dropped down the draw.

Where would the rustler be heading at night time — alone? The rider mused, hunkered in solitude beside the fire.

A sudden hunch hit him. He straightened and headed for the buckskin. Quickly, he cinched on the saddle and adjusted the bridle. Playing his hunch, he led the pony back to the fire, kicked the crackling sticks apart and stamped them out. Then he mounted and hit for Buzzard Gap.

Silence clothed the solitudes as the buckskin jogged steadily through the night. A full moon bathed the barrens with pale radiance, silvering the bare peaks that reared like giant sentinels

against the sky, peopling the arid flats with shadows and trans-
forming the twisted junipers into writhing specters.

When at last Harrigan emerged from the narrow portals of
the pass, he drew rein, eying the veiled mystery of the vast dun
valley below. If his hunch proved a dud, he considered, he would
have made a long, lonely night ride for no purpose, with a long
chance that Colorado would beat him back to the hideaway —
and fire awkward questions. The scarred rustler looked like he
could talk fast — with his guns.

For a moment, Harrigan battled an impulse to back-track,
then he shrugged and heeled the buckskin. Might just as well
play the hand out.

Hooves rasping upon rock and scattering loose shale, the
pony slid and slipped down the steep trail. Like a pallid star, a
faint light pricked through the grayness of the valley below and
the rider's heart skipped a beat. There was no other place of habi-
tation within an hour's ride, outside of his abandoned adobe at
Bubbling Spring. Someone was at the spring.

As the buckskin dropped lower, Harrigan saw that the yellow
beam came from a square window of the adobe. Cautious now,
he pulled the pony down to a walk, circling to approach his old
homestead behind the screen of the chaparral around the spring.

In the deep shadow of the spreading willows he stepped
down, tied the buckskin and hung his spurs on the saddle-horn.

The adobe lay fifty paces from the spring, with a stretch of
bare ground between. Midway, to his left, was a pole corral and
open-side barn.

Bent low, Harrigan injuned around the edge of the bare
ground, dodged behind the barn and slipped through the corral
rails. No sound came from the adobe, but, as he cattoed across
the corral, he sighted two ponies, tied on the further side. The
ponies' ears flipped up as he silently slid between the rails again,
out into the open. The adobe was not more than twenty paces
distant now.

He eyed the stretch of bare ground doubtfully. Once he left the shelter of the corral he would be plain in the moonlight. Facing him, the doorway of the adobe made a yellow rectangle from the light of a lamp within. Close by, the ponies were fidgetting nervously, and one was Colorado's pinto.

Hesitating no longer, he strode silently and swiftly ahead. The pinto nickered. Checking in midstride, Harrigan heard the jingle of spurs inside the doorway, Colorado's hoarse voice. He dropped flat. There was no time to retreat to the shelter of the corral behind him.

Colorado emerged from the doorway, head swivelling from right to left. Behind him, Harrigan recognized the bulk of Chunky Nabor. So the foreman was double-crossing his iron!

Flattened on the bare yard, Harrigan felt as conspicuous as the hump on a camel.

"Hell, they got a whiff of wolf scent!" ejaculated Chunky.

Colorado said nothing, just stood outside the doorway, peering around like an old hound questing for scent.

Again the pinto whickered. An answering whinny came back from the buckskin, tied beneath the willows. With a quick oath, Colorado grabbed a gun butt and started forward. He focussed Harrigan's flattened form. The moonlight gleamed on the blued steel of his arcing gun.

CHAPTER SIX

ARRIGAN thrust off the ground with desperate haste, grabbing for his iron as flame lanced from Colorado's gun. A slug sledge-hammered into his body, the impact twirling him around. He braced, flung a shot at Colorado's crouched form as the smoking gun came down again. The gunman rocked, his arm slackened and the weapon spilled from his fingers, clattering down upon the hard earth.

Chunky came into action now, side-stepping to clear his companion. A numbing paralysis was fast creeping over Harrigan. Already his left side was dead and weighing him down like lead. Chunky's gun flash stabbed the night as he gathered his fast-ebbing strength and hightailed for the corral behind him, twisting and dodging like a jackrabbit. A bullet droned past as he swayed upon rubbery legs. Another kicked dust between his feet. Then he squeezed between the corral rails and crawled towards the tied ponies. A quick side-glance showed Chunky darting for the shelter of the adobe, while Colorado's stubborn figure was silhouetted in the moonlight, right arm hanging limp, thumbing his lefthand gun.

Harrigan's crawling form was covered by the two tied ponies now. He rose and staggered, half bent, across the corral towards the spring. Blood ran warm down his left leg. Jaw locked, he drove his weakening body forward. He knew it was death if he went down.

The renegade chief shuffled sideways, but the fugitive was across the corral and in the shadows before Colorado cleared the ponies and his gun began blaring again.

Chunky peered around the angle of the adobe and whipped slugs across the corral. The pinto squealed and rose high, went down in a flurry of threshing hooves. As he dragged through the chaparral, Harrigan heard Colorado's acrid voice, hoarse with anger, cursing Chunky's careless gunplay.

He blundered around beneath the willows, stumbling and colliding with tree trunks in the gloom, while lead laced the shadows. It was seconds, but it seemed hours before he located the buckskin, hauled his bleeding body into the saddle and drove the steel home. Lips locked, he clung to the horn, his body sagging like an empty waterbag, while the pony pounded across the flats.

Far out on the plain, the blowing buckskin slackened speed. Harrigan still froze onto the horn. Mesquite, moon, stars spun around in a dizzy whirl. No sound disturbed the quiet of the plain save the wheezing snorts of the pony as it sucked air into its lungs.

Fighting to clarify his senses, the wounded rider slid to the ground, steadied against his mount and peeled off his shirt. It was wet and red. He slipped off his bandanna, wiped his sticky hands. Then he eyed his bloodied side. Colorado's slug had entered low down, below his ribs, smashed through and emerged above the buttock. A small, puckered hole, from which blood was flowing sluggishly, marked the point of impact, but his life blood was steadily draining from a gaping hole in the rear. He tore his bandanna into strips, plugged the holes as best he could, eased on his shirt and pulled himself into the saddle again.

At the pressure of his knees, the buckskin resumed its habitual jog-trot and he moved across the flats again, too weak to do more than stay in the saddle.

Blood was pooling on his saddle. He reached up to wipe off the sweat beading upon his forehead when a black fog blotted out the stars .... When his brain cleared he found himself lying upon a carpet of pungent sage. The buckskin was cropping close by.

He crawled towards the pony, gasped the dangling reins, hung onto a stirrup and wavered to his feet. His knees were as loose as well-oiled hinges and he was hard-put to prevent them buckling.

Around stretched the silvered range, overshadowed by the serried Dragoons, a vast emptiness, dim and desolate. Seemed he was close to the end of his rope, considered the fugitive wearily. It was plain he wouldn't last long in the sadle with an open wound. More riding would drain him dry of blood. His only chance was to find a hide-out and rest until the wound closed. And he must have water if he was to survive. There was no water closer than Bubbling Spring.

Twice he collapsed, panting, as he fought to get a leg across the saddle. At the third attempt he made it, but blood belched above his buttock. He wheeled the pony, heading back for the spring. Maybe he was riding to his death, but if dawn found him wandering across the open range the pitiless sun would finish him.

Vaguely, he was conscious that the adobe was deserted when he rode in, flopped across the pony's withers. A dead pinto lay by the corral. The buckskin halted at the spring. Its head dropped to drink and the sorely wounded man spilled off and sprawled in the dust.

The prickling rays of the rising sun stung him into consciousness. His head raised and he stared around with dulled eyes. The soft splash of water dribbling from the spring tantalized him. His tongue rasped over dust-caked lips. He hooked his fingers and dug the sharp toes of his riding boots into the dirt, inched forward until he could lap the cool water. Then he crawled, like a wounded animal, beneath the cover of a bushy greasewood.

Through the day he lay in the shade of the greasewood. His brain was crystal-clear but strength had seeped out of his body. Every slight movement was effort. Twice he dragged the few paces to the spring. The second time he collapsed midway back to the greasewood and lay in the sun glare. He felt no pain. A deep lassitude cloaked his senses. It was, he considered dreamily, a dandy way to die.

As the sun slanted westward, a shadow passed across his body. He rolled upon his back, squinting into the sky. A black buzzard had floated past, ragged pinions clear-etched against the blue. Another joined it. He watched as they circled lower — lower.

Weakened as he was, the instinct for survival was still strong. At sight of the buzzards the pleasant languor fled and a cold chill settled on the wounded man. He had seen men after the buzzards had worked on them. He fumbled for his gun. The barrel wobbled when he fired. At the report the buzzards rose higher, but they quickly dropped down again.

A renewed craving for life fastened upon the helpless man. He spurred his mind, fighting drowsiness. He could hear the buckskin cropping in the brush. Maybe he could straddle the pony again. But where could he ride? Death awaited him at the rustlers' hideout; Limpy Leeman was hunting him in Powwow; Bull Flint at the Turtle; Chunky Nabor at the ACC — enemies everywhere!

A wing brushed his face. His eyelids flicked up. The buzzards were thick now. They fluttered around, perched on the rocks of the spring and preened on the branches of the willows, staring with black, beady eyes.

He rolled over upon his belly, clawed his way back to the protection of the greasewood.

The sun set. His surroundings purpled, faded into obscurity. The buzzards were gone and a soothing quiet lay on the spring. The wounded man lay in semi-stupor. Then the night was filled with melancholy howling of coyotes. Beyond the corral they began snarling and snapping around the body of the dead pinto.

It wouldn't be long now, considered Harrigan dully. A bit chain tinkled at the spring. He levered his body up upon an elbow, whistled. Head outstretched, the buckskin nuzzled through the brush.

Powwow slept. The last poker game had broken up in The Double Eagle and the swinging oil lamps were dowsed. A cat slunk across Main Street and rats scurried around the stacked flour on the gallery of McArdle's Store.

A buckskin plodded slowly past the deserted hitch rails, turned at the vacant lot beside the saddler's and was checked at the cabin in the rear.

Its rider loosed his grip upon the horn, slid helplessly down upon a shoulder and lay in a huddled heap. The pony drifted off across the lot, heading for the horse trough beside the saloon. After awhile, the rider stirred, crawled laboriously towards the cabin door. He reached it, grasped the doorknob and raised, inch by inch, until he stood erect. With his free fist he pounded weakly upon the panel.

The door flung open and Ruby, hair streaming over her shoulders and shapeless in a faded red dressing gown, eyed her visitor, grabbing a sawed-off shotgun with both hands.

Her enraged glance ran over the teetering rider. "Dammit!" she flamed, "Don't I see enough drunks in The Double Eagle without having them around here? Skat! Or I'll fill you so full of buckshot they'll use you for a sieve."

The swaying man crashed down and lay across the threshold. Ruby swore again, stepped across the body and set the gun against the cabin. With distaste, she bent and began to drag the prostrate form away from the door.

A startled exclamation left her lips. Her grip suddenly loosened and she straightened, staring wide-eyed at her reddened fingers. Tensed, she turned the body over and knelt, sniffed and eyed the unshaven, dust-smeared features.

"My Gawd!" she muttered, "He's not drunk." She glanced quickly around, hesitated, then commenced hauling the unconscious man into her cabin.

The sun shone bright through curtained windows when Harrigan awoke. He attempted to sit up, but a branding iron seared deep into his back. So he lay quiet, his body heavy with lassitude, content to relax between the clean sheets of a comfortable bed. His brow creased as he eyed his strange surroundings. Silk dresses hung from pegs on the wall. Jars of cream and fancy bottles crowded a small dressing table. Small, high-heeled shoes were lined along the wall. His tired brain abandoned the problem and he slept again.

The opening of a door aroused him a second time. Incredulously, he stared at Ruby, the dance hall girl. Blonde hair stacked high, bare arms powdered and lips carmined, she slammed the door irritably and stood eying him as she might have eyed a burnt dinner or a run in a silk stocking.

"Howdy!" Harrigan could raise no more than a whisper.

"Howdy!" she blurted out, "A nice howdy this is — banging a girl up after midnight and passing out on her doorstep! My reputation's bad enough as it is. It'll sure be in shreds when this gets around."

He frowned, groping at elusive memories, "How come I got here?"

"I certainly didn't invite you!" she came back tartly.

He closed his eyes, still probing ineffectually into jumbled recollections — Colorado's gun spurting fire, the buzzards, snarling coyotes — a nightmare ride. "Reckon I musta rode here," he croaked, with disbelief.

"Why pick on me? Am I the only sucker in town?"

His lips quirked at the indignant curve of her red lips and the fire sparking in her eyes. "I reckon my pony's got good hawse sense, ma'am, and I'm sure thanking you for this bed."

Ruby sniffed, pulled a chair close and sat down beside him.

TOM WEST

"How do you feel — stranger?"

"They call me Yuma."

"Which is probably an alias as false as your black hair."

"I reckon it's showing kinda pale around the roots," he agreed. His eyelids closed. It was an effort to hold them open.

"How did you get that gunshot wound? There was no shooting in town last night."

"Lemme rest awhiles," he muttered wearily, "I'll talk plenty — later."

"Sure, Yuma!" Her voice softened as she rose, "I got to get back to the joint or Whitey will bust his corset strings." She set a jug and glass on the chair seat. "Drink this if you get thirsty. I'll fix some soup after awhile."

Around midnight, Ruby returned. She pinned a blanket across the cabin, screening the bed. Harrigan heard her shuckling her dance hall finery and when she brought the soup, her hair was coiled around her head and she wore a gingham house dress. Soft leather slippers flapped upon her feet.

"Ma'am," said the wounded man with appreciation, "I sure like you better thisaway."

"No one asked you what you liked," she flung back, irritably, "Why do I have to mother every stray pup?"

She sank on to the chair while he spooned the soup, "Gawd, how my dogs ache!"

Harrigan finished a second bowl of soup and sank back against the pillows. "Maybe it's time I talked, ma'am."

"It will help me decide if I should call the sheriff." There was an edge to her voice. It had been a tiring day in The Double Eagle.

"That means the rope f'r me," he said somberly. "Lissen!"

He told his story, holding back nothing, from the night of his partner's death, through the shooting of Cheyenne Dan to the fracas at Bubbling Spring.

The girl listened without a word. When he concluded, she said thoughtfully:

58

"Hap Harrigan! I've heard about you. There was something screwy about that shooting. There's been talk in the saloon."

"You wouldn't know —" began Harrigan, hope kindling in his eyes.

Ruby shook her head vigorously, "I don't know nothing. Something tells me it wouldn't be healthy to know — too much."

"Which don't help me any," he said bitterly.

"Mister, I've got trouble enough without shouldering yours. Right now I've qualified for the hoosegow for harboring a jail-breaker."

The wounded man eyed her curiously. Ruby looked softer, more womanly, without the paint and tinsel. She was good-hearted, too, even if her tongue was sharp. How come she hung around a joint like The Double Eagle?

"And get this, Yuma," she went on, "I want you out of here just as soon as you can sit a saddle. These floor boards are almighty hard and a girl deserves better than that when she's deadbeat after a day's work."

"Milking dollars out of ignorant cowpokes!" he jibed, then regretted his ill-timed humor. This girl has eased him out of the worse tight he was ever in.

"So what?" she snapped, "A girl's got to live. How would you get by, smarty, if you wore skirts?"

"Not by capering around a dance hall."

Her eyes flashed, "Do you think I fancy those dumb clucks pawing me? Do you think I like swallowing rotgut to keep them company? Or grinning like a monkey when I'm itching to rake their ugly maps with my fingernails? If so, you're crazy. At that, it beats pearl-diving in a hash house, and it sure pays better."

"Not in self-respect."

"Self-respect," she snorted, "'You make me tired, Yuma. Did you ever stand at a cook stove, ten hours a day, when it was so scorching hot you could fry your steaks on the tin roof? I did — in

Nogales. Did you ever wash dishes when it was so hot the horned toads died of apoplexy? I did — in Phoenix. Did you ever wait on table till your feet burnt like fire, your back was breaking and the marrow was sweated out of your bones? I did — in Tucson. Give me a dance hall! Maybe a girl does get mauled a bit, but she can slip plenty greenbacks into her stocking. And — damn you for a grinning ape — she can still keep her self-respect."

"Ruby," he said quietly, "You're all wool and a yard wide."

"If that's a compliment," she scoffed, "you certainly need practice. Now roll over and let me take a look at your side."

She ripped up a clean cloth and removed the old dressings. "Looks good," she announced, "I was scared I'd have to sober up that old whisky-freighter of a sawbones. Then the fat would have been in the fire."

Strength flowed back into the wounded man. By the end of the week, he was padding around the cabin, loosening up cramped limbs, when Ruby was over at The Double Eagle. He wanted out of there. Not only was it mighty embarrassing to use a girl's bed and share her cramped quarters, but it was dangerous, when the deputy sheriff's office was practically across street. But Ruby had stowed away everything he had, down to his boots, and he couldn't locate the bundle. His disguise was wearing thin, too. The hair dye was in a saddlebag and he had no idea where the buckskin had wandered. Maybe it was back at Bubbling Spring.

When he looked into Ruby's mirror he saw what appeared to be a disordered black wig set upon short blonde hair. He cropped it short with a pair of scissors and trimmed the mustache. The girl had brought him a good razor, too. She was a jewel!

One morning while he was engaged in an intensive search for his clothes, footsteps outside hurried him back to the bed, for no more than a shirt covered his long form.

Behind the blanket screen he hard a sharp, insistent rap at the door. It opened and spurs jingled. Helpless, Harrigan lay and listened. Never had he craved a gun more.

The blanket jerked down. Deputy Sheriff Limpy Leeman stood eying him, gaunt features expressionless. "Wal, ef it ain't Hap Harrigan to the life," said the deputy dryly. "With a busted beak, jest like the dodger sez. So yore shacking up with Ruby! Git outa there — you mangy coyote!"

CHAPTER SEVEN

A SILKEN FURY tornadoed through the doorway. Ruby, cheeks ablaze beneath her rouge, flung herself at the bony deputy. Her dark eyes seethed with fury. "You get out of here, Limpy Leeman," she shrilled, "No one's shacking up with me. Thet man's helpless, he was shot."

The deputy backed, fending off the crooked fingers raking furiously at his face and grabbing at her white arms. A swift scuffle and he had the panting girl pinned against the wall. His Stetson lay on the floor and blood beaded upon a leathery cheek.

Harrigan's bare legs dropped over the edge of the bed. Before he could leap to the rescue, Limpy threw the dishevelled girl aside and jerked his gun, "Hold it, Harrigan!" he grated.

The fugitive hesitated, staring into the muzzle of a Colt .45.

"Git back to The Double Eagle," Leeman told the girl curtly, "And you, Harrigan, slide inter yore duds!"

"Listen to me, Limpy!" Ruby's voice was under control now and sharp with emphasis. "Harrigan was framed. You know it — and I can prove it! Turn him in and I'll raise so much hell they'll run you out of town — on a rail."

Harrigan thought he detected a flicker of uncertainty in the deputy's deep-set eyes.

"You dribble like a drunk squaw," barked Limpy, "Vamoose!"

"So did Cheyenne before he left town," returned the girl complacently. "He dribbled enough to put you in Yuma, Limpy — and how they hate the sight of your ugly map around here!"

"Put ME in Yuma!" The deputy eyed her closely.

"Yes, you, and I know plenty of jaspers who'd be tickled to see you sweat. Now take him in and give them a laugh — damn you!"

"That" said Harrigan gravely, "is no language for a lady."

Ruby sniffed.

No emotion showed upon the mask of the deputy's bony features. Brittle silence held the cabin as he fixed the girl with unwinking stare, weighing her words. Harrigan was reminded of the expressionless eyes of the buzzards at Bubbling Spring. Then, abruptly the deputy dropped his gun into the holster, swung upon his heel and left the cabin.

No word passed between the two until the jingle of his spurs grew faint, died.

"Say, what did Cheyenne spill?" demanded Harrigan eagerly, jumping up from the bed, forgetful of his bare legs.

"How would I know?" answered Ruby with sudden weariness, "I never met the ape." She unlocked a trunk, tossed boots, pants and a new shirt towards the fugitive. "You better beat it — there's more in the trunk."

"So you bluffed the lobo!" chuckled Harrigan, gathering up his clothes. "He shut his face hard enough to bust his nut crackers." He sobered at a thought, "They won't —" he paused, searching for words.

"Rub me out? Nope, I got too many friends." Ruby patted her hair into place, crossed to the dressing table, picked up mirror and powder puff.

He draped a sheet around his legs and dropped onto the bed, eyes thoughtful, "How come Limpy got wise I was around?"

"I bought a couple of shirts at the store, and they picked up your pony, too, on Main Street. Limpy's smart — like a fox."

"Can I get holt of the buckskin?"

"Sure!" She dabbed powder on her face and neck. "It's in the corral behind the livery. Well, I got to get back to piano pounding." Her scarlet lips twisted as she eyed his bare calves, "So-long, legs!"

Harrigan, suddenly embarrassed, yanked the sheet into place. "Say, Ruby!" She stopped midway to the door. "I'm mighty sorry I got you in this jam. You're — aces high!"

"Forget it!" she shrugged, "I always was a sucker for a lame dog. That was a bonehead play, buying a man's shirts!" And she was gone.

Alone, Harrigan pondered on the deputy's amazing about-face as he pulled on his pants. It seemed that Limpy was tied in with Harry's killing tighter than he had figured.

Daylight was fading when he heard the clip-clop of hooves outside the cabin. Hand upon his gun, he pulled the curtain hastily aside and peered out. A rider was wheeling away, leaving his saddled buckskin ground-hitched. A bulging gunny sack was tied to the horn. Chuck, guessed the fugitive. Ruby forgot nothing. He clapped on his Stetson and strode outside.

By moonlight, he rode into Bubbling Spring. Nothing remained of the dead pinto but cleaned bones. Harrigan could not repress a shudder as he considered how close he had come to leaving his own at the spring.

He stripped saddle and bridle off the buckskin, hobbled it and rolled a cigarette, considering his next move. It seemed as though Ruby's threat had tied the deputy's hands, but he was no closer to uncovering his pard's killer than when he rode into Powwow. Limpy and Cheyenne were tied up in it, that was plain. And Chunky Nabor had backed Cheyenne's word. But they were tools in the hands of Bull Flint, the cowman who craved his water.

His thoughts drifted to the rustling gang, Colorado and his mysterious boss. Bull again, mused the fugitive, every crooked trail led back to him. Then he considered the raping of ACC range, where Chunky was double-crossing his Limey boss. Here was a chance to kick at Bull Flint — expose Chunky and clean up the rustlers. That would hit Bull where it hurt — in the pocketbook.

At sunup he kindled a small fire, spilled coffee from a paper sack into a tin can and set it on the coals. While it was heating he broiled some strips of beef on sticks and munched dry biscuit. Next he shaved, touched up hair and mustache with the black dye.

Feeling as spry as a two-year-old, he saddled his pony and headed north for the ACC. In a fold of the hills, he sighted the spread, slumbering in the morning sun. Cottonwoods stood spaced like sentinels in front of a large rambling timber-and-adobe ranch house, low-built, with a wide gallery. In the rear sat a long bunkhouse, big square barn, blacksmith shop and other buildings, grouped around a yard.

Behind the barbed wire of a hoof-chopped pasture, ponies nuzzled the sparse clumps of grama. In a separate pasture, a black trotted restlessly behind the wire, head held high. With a horseman's admiration, Harrigan drew rein and feasted his eyes on the animal. He had never seen better: long, muscular shoulders; flat straight back; small head and long deep barrel told of speed, stamina and breeding.

From habit he headed for the yard, then kneed the buckskin and pulled around in front of the house. Ordinarily, he would have dropped in at the bunkhouse, but on this trip he wanted to see the boss before Chunky saw him.

He stepped across the shaded gallery and knuckled a heavy plank door. A slightly-built youth in spotless white coat opened it.

"Boss around?" inquired Harrigan.

The young Mexican hesitated, eying his dusty range garb, then glimpsed his visitor's cold blue eyes. "Si, *señor*," he returned hastily, "I weel call the *Señor* Tailborne.

He was about to close the door when Harrigan pushed past and stepped into a spacious room. This was new territory. The rider eyed a massive rock fireplace, colorful Navajo blankets draped upon the adobe walls and the glossy pelts of bear and cougar that patched the hard-packed earth floor. A round table in the center of the room was littered with newspapers and magazines, while well-padded leather rockers were set invitingly around. This Tailborne hombre, he decided, did himself proud.

He restrained an impulse to hunker against the wall and carefully lowered himself into an upholstered armchair. He was considering the wide-spreading horns of a steer mounted over the fireplace when a discreet cough brought him to his feet. He turned and checked a quirk of the lips.

Moving languidly towards him was a tall, thin young fellow with slightly stooped shoulders and fine-drawn patrician nose. His high forehead carried a bored frown. Receding above it were waves of carefully brushed light brown hair. He was clean-shaven, except for a smudge of mustache upon his upper lip. An open-necked silk shirt, vivid scarlet bandana and gray cord riding breeches completed the ensemble. But the slightly dazed Harrigan gazed with rapt attention at a circle of glass, the size of a dollar, that by some magic stuck in front of the newcomer's right eye. A black silk ribbon drooped from it.

"How d'ye do?" drawled the stranger, "The name is Edgington-Tailborne, Reginald Edgington-Tailborne — hyphened."

"Yuma!" choked his visitor, grabbing a slackly extended hand, "Jest plain Yuma."

"Welcome to the ACC, Mr. Yuma!" His host carelessly cloaked a yawn. "Always glad to see a visitor. It's beastly boring in this barn and infernally hot outside."

He dropped into a chair and the monocle dropped, too. Harrigan's fascinated gaze followed it as it swung, pendulum-like, from the ribbon. With reluctance, he pulled his gaze away and looked into two eyes as blue as his own.

"Sit down, Mr. Yuma!" smiled the Dude, "Remove the weight from your legs, in the Western vernacular."

Harrigan sank onto the edge of a chair, searching for words. "Dandy black you got out there," he commented.

Quick enthusiasm drove boredom from the Dude's eyes. "My saddle horse, Blackie, Kentucky raised."

"Can't say I've seen a better."

"They don't come any better," said Edgington-Tailborne pridefully. Then Harrigan got around to the purpose of his call. "You rod the ACC?" he inquired abruptly.

"Well, er, I manage the ranch. My foreman, Mr. Nabor, handles the men and the stock. You might say that I act in an executive capacity, purely advisory, doncher know!" The Englishman pulled a briar pipe out of a pants pocket and commenced to stuff the bowl from a monogramed pouch.

"Jumping grasshoppers!" thought Harrigan, "What a cinch for Chunky!"

"How many cows you losing?" he asked, aloud.

The other glanced up, obviously startled at the question. "Comparatively few, old chap. There is some small diminution, I presume, from natural causes."

"I gamble you lost twelve hundred prime steers in the past month."

The Dude smiled indulgently, "Come, come! That's ridiculous, quite ridiculous, my dear fellow!"

"That's cold fact, mister," came back Harrigan coolly, "I helped rustle 'em!"

Reginald Edgington-Tailborne was not excited. He produced a block of sulphur matches, struck one and applied it to the bowl of his pipe. Then sank back into his chair and puffed casually, regarding his visitor's roughhewn features with amusement. "Tut, tut! I suppose you will have your little joke, old man, although to me this Western humor is really quite obtuse."

"I ain't funnin'," came back the rider brusquely. "At forty dollars a head at the stockyards, thet's most fifty thousand dollars. Ain't nothing funny about that!"

Amusement faded from the Dude's eyes. He straightened, "Do you mean to insinuate that twelve hundred cows have been deliberately stolen from this ranch recently?" Strangely, his lazy drawl had disappeared.

"Jest that!"

"And you were implicated in the theft?"

"I sure was!"

The Dude relaxed again, "Ridiculous and quite illogical! If you were involved, my dear fellow, you positively would not, er, tip your hand."

"I done split with the gang. Now listen, mister!" Harrigan told of the rustlers, the night riding, Chunky's meeting with Colorado at Bubbling Spring. When he was through, he knew from the bored expression upon the Dude's features that he was not believed. "Now call me a doggoned liar!" he challenged.

The Dude smiled gently, "Shall we say that you are a prevaricator with a whimsical sense of humor?"

"Maybe, except that I kin prove cows are leaking off ACC range like water out of a busted barrel."

"Perhaps you forget that these, raw, rustled cows, were branded — a mark of ownership quite difficult to remove, unless one skins the beasts," replied the other ironically.

Harrigan's patience was wearing thin. "B'gosh mister," he burst out angrily, "You don't know dung from wild honey! Ain't yuh ever heard of a blotched brand? And don't you keep a tally? Or do yuh jest set around and go broke?"

His earnestness apparently impressed the Dude. The latter coughed apologetically, "I must confess, old boy, that I am comparatively new to this perplexing country. I understand, however, that the animals are counted at roundup."

"Come roundup you won't have no cows to count."

Reginald Edgington-Tailborne was uneasy. That was apparent from the vigor with which he drew upon his pipe and the puzzlement in his eyes. "I shall consult with Mr. Nabor concerning these alleged peculations," he finally observed.

"Ain't you got the brains of a bumblebee? Chunky's hogswiggling yuh!"

"I have only your unsupported word, Mr. Yuma," came back the Dude with dignity, "the word of a confessed malefactor."

"So I'm a cockeyed liar!" Harrigan glowered at the dignified Englishman. An idea struck him, "I kin prove Chunky's as crooked as a corkscrew!"

"And I shall be delighted to consider the proof!"

Harrigan thought fast. " 'Member the loft in your hawse-barn?"

"I have never investigated the building, but I am familiar with its location."

"You should be!" growled the other. "Wal, after supper you sneak up into thet loft and stretch yore ears. Maybe I kin tole Chunky into the barn and git him to talk."

Edgington-Tailborne's nose wrinkled with distaste. "Most uninviting," he demurred, "and these cloak-and-dagger methods are positively abhorrent."

"Mister," challenged the other, "Is it worth, fifty, maybe a hundred thousand dollars to stick your snout in that loft?"

The Dude sighed. "I still suspect you are ragging me, but it shall never be said that an Edgington-Tailborne blanched at the call of duty. I am willing to conceal myself in the barn like a filthy spy if you will explain one thing."

"Such as?"

"Why you — a complete stranger — are so concerned with the welfare of the Arizona Cattle Company."

"I don't give a gordamn f'r the ACC, I jest hate Chunky's guts."

Harrigan rode around to the yard and stepped down at the trough. He watered the buckskin, loosened cinches and tied the pony to the rail. Then he hunkered on the shady side of the bunkhouse, rolled a smoke and set himself to wait and consider the boss of the ACC. It just didn't seem possible, he pondered, that there could be a jasper like that — outside of a Kansas City vaudeville show.

The day wore on and the punchers jingled in, two by two, watered their ponies, stripped off their rigs and racked saddles. Gradually, the number of lounging riders, perched on the top rail of the corral, hunkered around the yard, drifting in and out of the bunkhouse, grew as supper time drew close. Daylight was dimming when Harrigan's questing gaze fell on Chunky as the foreman rode in.

The harsh jangling of the cook's cleaver upon a suspended iron bar caused a stampede for the grub shack. Harrigan crowded in with the rest and excited no comment. A spare grub-liner or two were always dropping in to any sizable spread. Jostled by hungry waddies, he slid upon a bench at the lower end of a long trestle table. There was little talk as the ACC crew cleaned huge platters of sizzling steaks, boiled potatoes and beans, poured coffee from steaming pitchers and got down to the serious business of eating.

Harrigan watched Chunky, overflowing a straightback chair at the head of the table, from the corner of his eye. When the foreman scraped back his chair, he slipped outside, casually blocked Chunky's path as the foreman emerged.

"Big news — Colorado — horse barn," he muttered and pulled away before the startled Chunky could fire any questions. He was banking that the foreman had not recognized him in the moonlight fracas at Bubbling Spring.

Standing inside the big square doorway of the barn, he waited, eying the darkening yard, pin-pointed with glowing cigarettes as riders trickled out of the grub shack and drifted around.

Beside him, rough wooden steps slanted up to the loft, the floor of which was pierced with square holes, the length of the barn, through which feed could be forked to the boxes below. Rats scampered and squealed in the darkness. If the Dude was squeamish, considered Harrigan, he was having a bad time up there in the gloomy recesses of the loft.

He drew a deep breath and stamped out his cigarette as a blocky form was outlined in the doorway.

Chunky stepped close, his features a white blur in the fading light. "What's fazing Colorado?" His voice had a sharp, nasal twang.

"He wants another thousand head — right now or sooner."

"A thousand!" The foreman's voice rose high with surprise. "Heck, the canyon's full of beef right now. He done hazed off five-six hundred head this past week. Hell, he jest can't handle a thousand!"

Harrigan shrugged, "He says your dude boss is so doggoned dumb he wouldn't wise up if you freighted the ranch house through the Gap." His lips quirked as he thought of the concealed Limey above — that remark was for his special benefit.

Chunky pushed closer, staring up into the taller rider's face. "Say!" suspicion sharpened his voice, "What's yore moniker? I ain't lamped you around the hideout, but I swear I heard yore voice somewheres."

"Wyoming," came back Harrigan nonchalantly, "I ain't been stringing along with the boys f'r more than a week."

"How come Colorado didn't use Red?"

"He ain't got back from Mesa."

The rustle of straw was plain in the loft above. Chunky's head jerked upward, a curse ripped from his lips as his right hand clamped on a gun butt. "What's the shenanigans?" he snarled.

"You're through, you dirty double-crosser," rapped out Harrigan. The muzzle of his gun prodded the squat foreman's belly, bulging over his leather belt.

"Reach!" growled the rider, and lifted the bewildered Chunky's gun. His voice raised, "Hey, Limey, you around?"

"Rather! Battling vermin in this infernal Black Hole of Calcutta. I swear a beastly rat nipped my nose," came a smothered reply from above.

"Better drop down!"

A match scratched. There was a faint glow at the head of the stairway and the rungs creaked as Edgington-Tailborne's once immaculate form was revealed in the yellow light of the stable lamp he carried. Wisps of straw clung to his silk shirt and cord breeches; dusty cobwebs festooned his hair and acute annoyance simmered in his blue eyes.

Even so, he retained his dignity. Setting the lantern down, he adjusted his monocle and surveyed the scowling Chunky.

"What have you to say for yourself, my good man?" he inquired icily.

The foreman achieved a sickly grin, "Aw, boss, we was jest funnin'."

"I suspected as much!" He turned to the astounded Harrigan. "Really, I must say you carry skylarking to ridiculous extremes. After all, there is a limit, doncher know! Put that lethal weapon away and go about your business, Mr. Yuma. You, too, Nabor. I consider the prank nauseating."

Harrigan's jaw slackened with amazement, "Jehoshaphat!" he gulped, "This ain't no play-acting!"

As his captor's gaze switched to the indignant Dude, Chunky whirled his plump form with catlike agility and flung himself at Edgington-Tailborne. Arms and legs flurried in the gloom, as the Dude sprawled headlong. Harrigan held his fire, fearful of plugging the ACC boss. Then the Dude was spread on the plank floor, while the foreman darted away into the darkness.

Harrigan jumped over the prostrate Edgington-Tailborne in pursuit. But Chunky's thick form had merged with the shadows of the yard. He holstered his gun and returned to the Dude, as the latter slowly raised his shoulders off the floor and blinked around with bewildered eyes. His lips were tight with anger.

Derisively, Harrigan watched the disconsolate Edgington-Tailborne scramble to his feet, pull out a spotless white handkerchief and wipe straw and dirt off his smooth cheeks. But when he spoke, the rider's voice was soft, "Ain't we got fun!"

CHAPTER EIGHT

EGINALD Edgington-Tailborne straightened his dishevelled form, fumbled for his monocle and turned his back upon Harrigan's derisive grin.

He was well through a cigarette when the Dude's form again loomed before him. "The ruffian has disappeared, completely disappeared!" Annoyance riffled the Englishman's voice. He paused as Harrigan said nothing, then coughed apologetically, "I am beginning to suspect that your allegations may have sound foundation. Will you join me in a whisky and soda, Mr. Yuma?"

"A little coffin varnish wouldn't come amiss," agreed Harrigan, rising, "but nix on the soda. My tapeworm ain't got an educated thirst."

The white-coated Mexican youth had lit several brass oil lamps, bracketed around the living room walls. In response to the Dude's summons, he brought in a bottle of Scotch whisky, soda water and glasses; pulled a small side table forward and set out the refreshments. Edgington-Tailborne collapsed into the depths of a rocker. "What a ghastly experience!" he murmured, tilting the bottle, "Say when, old top!"

"Jest fill her up," requested Harrigan gravely, "I stutter!"

In comfortable silence, they sipped their drinks.

"Smooth as silk," volunteered Harrigan, at the Dude's cocked eyebrow, "but it lacks that burning sensation—I guess the snake musta crawled out. Wal, d'ye still figure I'm hurrahin' yuh?"

"No," conceded the Dude, "I must admit the evidence indicates that Mr. Nabor has a guilty conscience, else why would he beat a precipitate retreat and persist in eluding me?" He pulled out his pipe, eyed the bowl dolefully as he stuffed it, "His dereliction places me in a most unpleasant dilemma. Those men outside, undoubtedly diamonds in the rough, persist in regarding me with more amusement than respect. With Nabor gone I am at a complete loss." He sighed and poured another drink. "My relatives in England have considerable capital invested in this ranch. Imagine their consternation when Reggie— the hardy adventurer, the doughty pioneer—reports that he has mislaid all their bally cows. The mere thought is nerve shattering."

"To cut it short, you need a foreman."

"Without one," agreed the Dude plaintively, "I am lost."

"There's one setting right here!"

The Dude blinked, smiled tiredly, "You're pulling my leg, I fear, Mr. Yuma. Please desist! My nerves are, er, a little rattled."

"You won't find a better," persisted Harrigan.

"But, my dear fellow," expostulated the Dude, "You have no references, you are a confessed rustler, you associate with disreputable characters. How could I possibly entrust this valuable ranch and the fortunes of the Edgington-Tailbornes, to such a man. The very idea is devastating."

He raised a languid hand as Harrigan opened his mouth to reply, "Not that I underestimate your personal qualities. Perish the thought! You have a ruggedness, a strength of character that is admirable. Yes, indeed!"

"Limey!" Harrigan's voice was patient, "You got to learn plenty, and you got to learn fast. Bull Flint, the biggest cowman in Vulture Valley, got his start with a running iron — which is rustling. Around here we judge a man by what he's got in his craw, not in his jeans. And we don't give a damn f'r ancestors. I reckon we all come down out of the trees — way back. You're on the spot. Ef you don't smash Colorado, he'll smash you. Now I got an idea!"

He paused and jerked out his sack of makin's. "Chunky u'll hightail to the hideout, squawking like a stuck pig. They'll figure you'll bust the breeze to the sheriff and maybe come back with a posse. So their play is to get when the gettin's good. Chances are Colorado got another ear in the bunkhouse. I spotted Frenchy at supper, he always did linger on the wrong side of the law. Oncet the Lazy H most hung him up to dry.

"You spread word at sunup you want to tally the herd for losses, and have the boys round up your beef at Smooth Water. I'll stake my saddle Colorado's wise afore sundown. Then he'll jump right in to gather a wad of them cows."

"Good heavens, man!" ejaculated the Dude, aghast. "Are you suggesting that we lure the ruffians on to ACC range? Whatever would we do?"

"Clean the bustards up!" came back Harrigan carelessly, "You've got twelve, fourteen waddies in yore bunkhouse. Colorado can't muster more'n eight." His voice brittled, "Don't tell me you're scairt of the odds!"

The scion of the Edgington-Tailbornes sat dumb with dismay as the meaning of his companion's words sank home. He had been schooled to an habitual respect for law and order, with a policeman on every corner to handle malefactors and a stern judge to caution those who stepped on the grass. The thought of taking the law into his own hands, to kill or be killed, smacked of anarchy or worse.

"But that would be breaking the law," he quavered.

Harrigan grinned. "The deputy at Powwow is so doggoned crooked he could crawl through a cactus patch — so he don't count. The sheriff at Apache City is fifty-sixty miles away — and he don't give a damn!"

The Dude still hesitated, nervously stroking his mustache. "I am frightfully sorry," he decided at last, "but I really cannot countenance open warfare. This Colorado fellow's indiscretions are strictly a matter for the law. There are prisons for such men. But for us to ambush and kill, without official authorization, why, it's simply unthinkable!"

Harrigan drew a deep breath, "Would you fight if Colorado raided the ranch?"

"Certainly, in self-defense."

"Ain't this self-defense?"

"Now you're quibbling!" accused the Dude.

Harrigan shrugged and poured another drink. He was beginning to fancy the Scotch. It packed a wallop, though it slid down like cream. Kind of delayed action, he mused. He had been hoping the Dude would pack a wallop, too.

The Mexican entered in silent zapatos, a rawboned waddy in a faded hickory shirt jingling behind him.

Edgington-Tailborne rose, polished his monocle and focussed it upon the newcomer.

"Hate tuh butt in, boss!" The waddy's voice was husky and he was obviously ill at ease, "But yore black's missing."

"Missing!" almost wailed the Dude.

"Wal, Chunky left thet paint of his'n behind."

"And stole Blackie?"

"It kinda looks thataway."

"The dirty, despicable thief!" The Dude's voice vibrated with feeling. He swung towards Harrigan, who noted with inward elation the anger that supplanted indecision in his blue eyes and the straightening of his stooped shoulders. Seemed like the Dude was stirred up at last.

"Did you hear that, Yuma? The cur stole Blackie!"

"I wouldn't put it beyond him."

"But it's unthinkable, outrageous!" The Dude waved the open-mouthed Mexican and poker-faced waddy away. Then he transferred his attention to Harrigan again. "Do you still wish to become foreman of the ACC and eliminate these — parasites?"

"Ef you give me a free hand."

"Absolutely!"

"It's a deal!" It was curious, pondered the rider, how you could get action out of a hombre, if only you prodded him in the right spot. Who'd have figured this citified son would get so choused up over his saddle pony?

The Dude was rapidly recovering his aplomb. He resumed his seat and relit his pipe. "There is, of course," he observed "the matter of remuneration."

"You name it!" said Harrigan offhand, "I ain't in this f'r dinero."

When Harrigan pulled back the straight-back chair and took Chunky's seat at breakfast he apparently drew no more attention than he had when he slid into the grub line the previous evening. But he knew that every man on each side of the long table was weighing him and pondering the new development. Chances were they all knew the ACC was being rustled blind. He would have given plenty to know how many were tied up with Colorado.

He said nothing until the waddies had filled up on flapjacks and bacon. When the tobacco sacks and cigarette papers came out, he rapped against his mug with a spoon.

Eighteen heads swivelled and eighteen pairs of eyes appraised him with blank disinterest. "Boys," he said evenly, "Chunky done lit out with the boss's saddle hawse, which makes him a hawse thief. I'm setting the saddle from now on and I got a hunch ACC cows have been strayin', in chunks. The boss craves a tally, so we start gatherin' pronto, throwing 'em onto the flat at Smooth Water." He paused, his glance, cold and challenging went around the table, "Ef any of you jaspers differ from my notion thet Chunky Nabor stinks, now's the time to loosen his yawp."

There was silence, suddenly broken by a loud "phat" as a long-geared rider, known as Frenchy, spat forcibly. Frenchy had a tangle of greasy black hair, drooping mustachios and a surly mouth. Harrigan eyed him.

"Wal, what's eatin' you?" he asked softly.

"I'm quittin', here and now," announced Frenchy truculently, "I don't crave to ride for no tailor's dummy, nor no two-bit foreman."

Harrigan's chair crashed upon its back. Five quick strides and he was beside Frenchy. The long-geared rider straightened quickly, swung to face him. Punchers on either side hastily slid along the bench.

The new foreman's left hand dabbed forward and fastened upon Frenchy's shirt front. He gathered a fistful of the cloth and jerked the surly-mouthed man across the bench, hit him hard beside his lantern jaw with his bunched right fist. As Frenchy swayed, he jabbed him in the ribs with a short vicious left, then stepped back. The long-geared rider staggered backward, pawing at his holster. Hand poised above his gun butt, Harrigan — eyes hard as blued steel — watched him. "Jerk thet gun," he warned, "and I'll jest naturally ventilate your thinkbox — it needs a whiff of fresh air."

But Frenchy had no stomach for hot lead. Muttering, he edged towards the door. "Ef you're around when I come out," Harrigan threw after him, "I'll collect enough of your hide to make a saddle cover."

He turned to the silently watching crew, "Rattle your hocks, boys, we gotta get busy."

At sundown, he headed for Buzzard Gap. On the flats below the Gap his deserted homestead stood gray and desolate in the fading light, its fences sagging and corral weed-grown. Didn't take long, he pondered, for a spread to fall apart. He dropped down, watered his pony at the spring and filled his waterbag. He didn't see the man who squinted curiously at him through a square window of the adobe.

Pulling away from the spring, he jogged over broken, rising terrain, towards the Notch. As darkness closed in, he tied the buckskin in a tangle of chokeberry, shucked his spurs and legged up the bouldery slopes until he located a hideout amid a huddle of rocks. Below him, the trail angled down from the dark notch of the Gap. If his hunch was right and Frenchy was tied in with the rustlers, Colorado would have had another visitor — a visitor bearing news that should toll the renegade into Vulture Valley as surely as a covey of plump quail would draw a fox into a thicket.

Scarcely had he set his waterbag on the ground when iron-shod hooves rang on the trail and his eyes followed Chunky's dim form as the ex-foreman, forking the Dude's black, reined down into the valley. Tight with anticipation, he waited for the remainder of the gang, but when false dawn glimmered against the eastern horizon, no more riders had emerged from the Gap. Harrigan stretched stiff limbs, knuckled the sleep out of his eyes and stumbled down to his pony.

While he slept in the bunkhouse, dust plumes streaked the clear air over the range as punchers combed the hills and draws, hazing bellowing steers towards Smooth Water.

Again, Harrigan hit for the Gap at nightfall, still convinced that a raid was due. He circled to take in Smooth Water, where four punchers held the ever-growing herd on the flat, warned them to hightail at the first sign of trouble and dog the herd. There was no percentage in throwing away lives.

A brittle expectancy held Harrigan when he hunkered down in the nest of rock again. Some intangible intuition told him that the rustlers would ride through the Gap that night. He could feel warning of impending action in his bones. Nerves wire-tight, he watched the trail. Never did the hours crawl so slowly. Twice, debris, sifting down from the heights above and spilling upon hard rock, brought him to his feet. At last, the sound for which he had been waiting so long came sharp and distinct to his ears — the click of ironshod hooves upon rock.

Tensed, he watched eight riders, no more than shadows floating past in the night, drop silently down trail. There was no mistaking Colorado's squat outline in the lead. He picked out Red's jaunty figure, but there was no sign of Chunky's broad bulk.

The string of riders wound down the coiling trail and dissolved into the darkness.

Harrigan descended behind them and raced for his pony. Colorado and his gang had ridden into the trap. Now he had to spring it.

Holding the buckskin down to a trot to conserve its strength for work ahead, Harrigan headed back to the ranch. He figured he had time to spare. The rustlers would have their hands full trailing the big herd gathered at Smooth Water and a bellyful easing it through the narrow Gap.

The ranch was darkened when he rode in. He lit a stable lantern, set it on the bunkhouse table and moved down the bunks, shaking and slapping sleeping men into wakefulness. In a few minutes, a dozen sleep-drugged waddies were struggling into pants and yanking on boots, trying to grasp what it was all about. Their eyes opened wide at the new foreman's curt order, "Saddle up! Pack Winchesters and plenty shells."

Into the confusion that boiled around the corral gate, where sleepy, swearing riders led their roped ponies out of dust-fogged darkness, cinched on saddles and dodged flying hooves, a tall, thin rider in denim pants, gray shirt and pearl-gray Stetson, packing a smooth, saddle upon his shoulder, wormed through the press to Harrigan's side.

"Pardon me, old chap," he drawled, "Could I be provided with a bally horse?"

"This ain't no place f'r you, boss," remonstrated the new foreman, "Lead's due to fly, aplenty. You ain't cut out for this sort of thing. 'Sides," he added slyly, "It's strictly illegal and agenst the law."

"As manager of the ACC," reiterated Edgington-Tailborne firmly, "I demand a horse."

"But you ain't heeled," protested Harrigan.

The Dude triumphantly pulled a derringer out of a pants pocket.

Harrigan stifled further protest, there was no time for whittle-whanging. "Say, throw this mustard plaster on a spare pony f'r the boss," he told a nearby puncher.

The Dude beamed impartially upon horses and horsemen, "This is really quite thrilling, doncher know, the wild west at its best."

Harrigan grinned, without amusement, "You ain't seen nothing — yet."

A compact block of riders jingled across the swales towards the Gap. As they rode, Harrigan told tersely of the rustlers who were even then cutting ACC beef out of Smooth Water. "Ef any of you rannies," he concluded, "wants out — he kin beat it right now, and no questions asked." But no one pulled rein.

Through the quiet night pricked the report of a shot, mumbling away into the hills. A faint crackling salvo followed.

"I told them jaspers to hightail," growled Harrigan irately.

Ahead, the Gap reared its notched head and the pinnacles and escarpments of the mountain wall gleamed white in the moonlight. Harrigan led the cavalcade down into an arroyo. Leaving his men below to enjoy a smoke and tighten cinches, he clambered up the steep, sandy bank and sat on the rim, feet dangling, and watched the pallid plain.

It came through the night like the rumble of distant thunder — the deep-pulsating reverberation of a herd on the move. Soon Harrigan's straining eyes focussed the rustled beef, drifting across the flats like a dark, curved cloud, slanting back from horns on either end. Busy specks that were riders darted up and down the flanks of the herd, others pressed on the drag. Colorado was no piker, considered the watcher, he had cleaned out the entire flat.

Now the bellowing of steers, the sharp clack of colliding horns, the shrill yippees of the rustlers were plain, while beneath everything ran the deep, drumming monotone of the herd's ponderous advance.

This was it, thought Harrigan, and slid down into the arroyo. Quickly, he gathered the eager waddies around him and gave his orders. "Remember, you fellows," broke in the Dude's voice, "A hundred dollars gold to the man who recovers Blackie."

Riding point, a startled rustler gaped as a string of riders spewed out of the plain and streaked down upon him. Scarcely had his gun thundered a warning, when the attackers split into two parties, one sweeping down each flank of the herd.

He was wheeling his pony to cut back when a slug took him. In seconds his body was trodden into pulp by the sharp hooves of panicky steers.

Harrigan's pony stretched into a mad gallop. He whirled past the sea of horns and dust-swathed bodies that was the herd, a knot of yelling, spurring punchers pressing behind him. More guns flared ahead, as shadowy forms hurtled towards them.

"Spread out!" yelled Harrigan over his shoulder. Bending low, he rowelled the buckskin towards the nearest flash. The herd was milling in confusion now, churning up a pall of choking dust. Around it, guns boomed and men whirled sweated ponies amid darting patterns of gun flame. Harrigan thumbed his bucking gun again and again at cursing riders who loomed out of the crimson-stabbed gloom and as quickly disappeared. Then the herd stampeded. In a flash it was high-tailing across the plain — a thundering torrent of fear-crazy animals — crushing everything in its path. Plunging like gray ghosts through the drifting dust, ACC waddies quested for the surviving rustlers. But those that remained alive had vanished.

The dust began to settle and Harrigan gathered his men. When he tallied the exalting crew, two were missing and four nursed bullet wounds. One night guard, he learned, had been downed at Smooth Water; another puncher had taken a slug squarely between the eyes. A search over the hoof-chopped ground uncovered the remains of five rustlers, among them Colorado, his lined features implacable, even in death.

The four wounded punchers, none seriously hurt, jogged off for town at an easy gait, while the remainder of the crew headed back to the ranch. The Dude, hatless and dust-daubed, strove ineffectually to cloak his excitement beneath his habitual mask of boredom. He pulled up to Harrigan's stirrup as they rode beneath the stars, "Quite a glorious victory, what? Messy, but exhilarating, quite exhilarating! What a letter I shall write home!"

"Git to use that gamblers' gun?"

"Get to use it!" echoed the Englishman, indignation strong in his voice, "I emptied and reloaded until I ran out of cartridges. The barrel became so infernally hot it burnt my fingers."

"Thet sure warn't lawful," said Harrigan soberly. "You got no legal right tuh kill them poor fellers."

"One must protect one's own!"

"Whyfore does the country pay a sheriff and a scad of deputies?"

"The deputy in Powwow is quite useless and the sheriff — why, I believe you are pulling my leg!"

Breakfast over, the crew lounged around, chewing over the events of the night. Harrigan figured they had earned a day's lay-off. The Dude was sleeping. Then every man galvanized into alert wariness as six strange riders cantered into the yard.

From the top rail of the corral, Harrigan blinked as he recognized Limpy Leeman's bony frame. What trouble was brewing now? He jumped down and came forward to meet the deputy, as Leeman awkwardly swung his stiff leg out of the saddle.

"You got plenty gall bracin' me here," grunted Harrigan, "I got ten men who u'll side me with lead."

"I'm packing a warrant," Limpy hooked thumbs in his gun-belt and returned Harrigan's cold stare.

"The blood money would buy a right smart headstone."

For a moment the deputy's gaunt face was blank, then it crinkled into a parody of a grin, "This ain't on the old charge, Harrigan. This is something new. I'm arrestin' yuh f'r the murder of Chunky Nabor in Powwow, night afore last."

"Chunky murdered!"

"You should know — shot through the back."

"You're loco. I was out here on the spread."

"Kin yuh prove it?"

Harrigan thought fast. He had spent the night before last alone at Buzzard Gap. "Sure I can!" he bluffed.

"Then prove it tuh the judge!" The deputy sidestepped, reached for Harrigan's holstered gun. The foreman twisted around, clapping his hand upon the butt.

"Reach!" grated a voice. Harrigan looked up — into the muzzle of a Winchester, slanted across the horn of a posse-man's pony.

CHAPTER NINE

Tension tightened in the ACC yard. The possemen were fingering their Winchesters. Two waddies erupted out of the bunkhouse, buckling on gunbelts, while other waddies scuffed dust as they closed in upon the intruders, jaws ugly. Deputy Sheriff Leeman was no more popular on the range than he was in town. Blood still hot from the fracas with the rustlers, the punchers were ripe for trouble.

Harrigan sensed that one shot would set off a bloody melee. An itchy finger and the ranch yard would be laced with lead. He curbed his quick impulse to resist arrest. "Hold it, boys!" he yelled, "There's no trouble. I'll be back."

The sun was high when the possemen and their prisoner stirred the dust of Main Street. Powwow drowsed, showing no more signs of life than a bonneted woman entering McArdle's Store, a scattering of ponies outside The Double Eagle, squatting Mexicans nodding beneath the plankwalk canopies. Beneath the faded canvas awning of The Powwow Hotel, a burly man in city clothes, swinging a silver-topped Malacca cane, watched the riders drift by. His spade beard was neatly trimmed and his square jaw was closed upon a fat cigar. A hawk's nose arced from his features. Something in his stance stirred memories in the stony-faced prisoner's mind. Maybe a drummer or cattle buyer from Kansas City, he guessed.

In the law shack, he emptied his pockets and surrendered his money belt. Limpy scratched out a receipt.

"When do I get a hearing?" demanded the prisoner.

"Cain't say 'til I get word from the sheriff. Reckon I'll hev to pack yuh to Apache City."

"Another lousy frame-up!" commented Harrigan bitterly.

"Thet's what they all say!"

"What's the evidence?"

"You were seen at Bubbling Spring the night afore, and so was Chunky. Seems like you rode to town."

"There was no one at Bubbling —" began the prisoner heatedly, then stopped, ready to bite off his tongue. There went his alibi.

"And you never left the spread!" mocked Limpy. He hustled his prisoner through a rear door into a passageway. Two cells, with heavy plank doors, opened on each side. A small peephole was cut in each door.

Limpy swung open the door of the first cell and Harrigan stepped inside. The door slammed behind him and a padlock clicked. He looked around drearily, at the thin straw mattress on the bench bed, the bucket in the corner, the scribbling on the walls, and a dull hopelessness possessed him. Once again he was behind the bars, and no chance of release. If they failed to fasten Chunky's murder upon him, they'd send him back to Yuma as an escaped convict.

He stretched slackly on the straw mattress. Seemed like Limpy was scared to pick him up on the old charge, so he had trumped up a new one.

Why? The answer to that was plain — either for revenge or to cover up this new killing. But how did Limpy know he couldn't produce an alibi for that night? He must have been mighty sure of himself or he wouldn't have sworn in a posse and ridden out to the ACC. Why had Chunky been bushwhacked, anyway? Harrigan sighed and gave it up. It was all too deep for him.

The clink of spurs in the passageway outside roused him to attention. He sat up as the door rasped open and the big citified man he had sighted outside the hotel bulled in. "Upon my soul," boomed the visitor, in a deep, hearty voice, "it is indeed saddening to behold such a fine young fellow in the hands of the law. 'The brain may devise laws for the blood, but a hot temper leaps over a cold decree.' " He swung around to the sardonic deputy, "Shakespeare," he intoned majestically.

Then Harrigan knew. It was Slick Sam, a mellowed Sam, with blond hair and a blond beard.

Sam's left eyelid dropped swiftly at the recognition in the prisoner's eyes. With a flourish he whisked a white card from a vest pocket. "The name is Cyrus K. Lockridge," he boomed. Harrigan glanced at the neat black engraving:

Cyrus K. Lockridge
Investments
Chicago

"I am happy to meet you again, sir," continued the visitor, "but not in a prison cell. You may not remember me, but I have vivid recollections of your valued assistance when toughs assailed me in Tucson."

"I got you placed, Mister Lockridge," drawled Harrigan. "Take a seat, ef you can find one."

Sam pivoted towards the deputy, standing wooden by the cell door. He fished out a ten-dollar gold piece and dropped it into a pocket of the lawman's dangling vest, "I wish to converse a few minutes with this unfortunate young man, sheriff. I feel I am in his debt. Your indulgence will be greatly appreciated."

"You pack a gun?" grunted the deputy.

"For self-protection in this wild country." Sam slipped a Colt .45 from beneath his coat and extended it with a bow.

Limpy took the weapon and slammed the cell door.

"So they picked you up!" Sam rolled the cigar between his lips, his gaze sweeping the prisoner's trail-stained garb.

"Not on the reward dodger. Limpy done fastened a new killin' on me now."

"A new killing? That would be the body found by the creek." Sam dropped on to the mattress beside Harrigan. " 'Trouble is to man what rust is to iron,' from the German! Now tell me your story, brother, from the beginning, omitting nothing that may be of consequence."

Harrigan related his misadventures in detail, from Harry Hartstone's killing to the latest charge.

"So our dour-faced deputy is wise to your identity," commented Sam thoughtfully, "yet he held his hand when threatened by your — friend. The trouble seems to revolve around the section of land you hold at Buzzard Gap."

"Sure," agreed the prisoner dolefully, "I was framed f'r that — Bull Flint craves my water."

"And the banker craves it, but not for the water," mused Sam. "There is more to this than you think, brother. You may not realize that eastern capital is awakening to the possibilities of this great untapped West; that schemes are afoot, backed by unlimited capital, to build more railroads from coast to coast, and that Buzzard Gap offers the only feasible route across the Dragoons for fifty, perhaps a hundred miles."

"Heck, it don't mean nothing to me!"

"What is more tragic than ignorance?" groaned Sam. "Cannot you see that your land blocks the Gap? Is your brain so addled that you cannot perceive that you may be sitting upon a gold mine?"

"Right now I'm setting in a cell. Git me out of this tight and the land's yours — for free!"

Sam smiled benignly, "Now light dawns upon our joint financial horizon! Deed me the land, brother, and we will split fifty-fifty whatever recompense the fates may deem fit to bestow upon us. In your uncultured hands I fear that holding is more liability than asset."

Keys rattled outside the cell. Sam slipped a stubby derringer beneath the mattress, "Pack that in your boot top, brother. It is a potent persuader."

He was standing by the door when it opened, his features clothed with a benevolent smile.

In the front office, Sam dropped into a straight back chair beside the deputy's battered desk. "I fear, Sheriff," he remarked affably, "that there has been a miscarriage of justice, which you will undoubtedly hasten to rectify. 'One hour in doing justice is worth a hundred in prayer,' from the Arabian!"

"I don't git yuh!" The deputy eyed his self-possessed and well-clad visitor suspiciously.

"It is very plain," Sam's piercing gaze probed him. "I understand a man was murdered on Tuesday night and you suspect Yuma. Let us review the facts! Yuma rode from Bubbling Spring to the ACC ranch shortly after dark and remained at the ranch throughout the night. He states that he can produce a dozen witnesses to swear to this. Further, Sheriff, I have some little capital and also considerable influence in Washington. I intend to see that justice is done." He smiled expansively, "Indeed, I feel quite a paternal interest in the young man, seeing that he has been good enough to deed me his holding."

"Not Bubbling Spring!" Surprise was reflected in the deputy's voice.

"Precisely, the entire six hundred and forty acres," returned Sam complacently. "Quite a minor transaction, dovetailing with more comprehensive plans. I might even, Sheriff, be able to put you in line for something good." He stood up, beaming, "I shall await Yuma's release — there is nothing to be gained by holding him. Nothing," he repeated significantly. "Good day, Sheriff!"

Jauntily swinging his cane, he stepped majestically out upon the plankwalk.

A few minutes later, from the convenient cover of a shadowed alley, he watched the deputy limp rapidly across the street and disappear behind the glass-panelled doors of the bank. Mobile lips twisting with amusement, the confidence man dropped into The Double Eagle for a quick two-fingers. Then he too, made a beeline for the bank.

Behind the counter, a clerk, wearing a suit that had seen better days, was munching a sandwich. He quickly dropped it into the cash drawer at sight of the customer, wiped a smudge of mustard off his chin. While he waited, dulled eyes downcast, Cyrus K. Lockridge's searching gaze took in his stooped shoulders, hollow cheeks spotted scarlet, and sunken chest. Lunger, he registered. With a spacious wave of the hand he indicated the white-painted wooden walls the varnished floor the huge antiquated iron safe set behind the counter. "Crude," he murmured, "but sound — I hope!"

"We have that reputation," came back the clerk indifferently.

"Quite so!" smiled Sam, "I would like to make a small deposit, to draw against for incidentals." He pulled a fat roll from a pants pocket and carelessly peeled off ten $100 bills. Placing one of his crisp white business cards upon the rustling greenbacks, he pushed them across the counter.

At sight of the name, the clerk darted a quick glance at the new depositor. With muttered apologies, he scuttled for the closed door of a side office. Painted on the panel were the words, JUSTUS HORRMAN, PRESIDENT.

The clerk bobbed out again, "Would you step inside," he requested, "Mr. Horrman would like to meet you."

"With pleasure!" boomed Sam. The fish, he considered with satisfaction, was nosing at the bait.

The clerk raised a leaf at the end of the counter. Sam stepped through, knuckled the door ceremoniously and turned the knob. He had already acquainted himself with Justus Horrman's background. Old-timers remembered his father, a poverty-stricken nester with a hungry brood. Justus, the eldest, padded four miles to town in his bare feet each day to do odd jobs around the store.

The nester family drifted away, but the boy stuck. He slept in a shed, lived on store pickings, hoarded every dime of his meager wages. Somehow, he acquired a scraggy mule. Sam Hayes, the storekeeper, allowed him to take out fancy goods, ribbons, cheap jewelry, on credit, to peddle from ranch to ranch. In a year he was a full-fledged range peddler with two good Missouri mules hitched to a band wagon. Somehow, folks weren't surprised when he took over the store at Hayes' death. Nor when, ten years later, he moved over to the bank.

Now in his fifties, Justus Horrman was a man without vices and without friends...beyond his dollars. He neither drank, smoked nor gambled, but he owned the saloon. It was a money-maker!

Horrman's qualities stuck out like a porcupine's quills, considered Sam, bowing in the doorway. His dark coat was frayed at the cuffs and pressed until the cloth shone. His pinched face was precise and rigidly controlled. His lips were pursed as though held by a drawstring and his thin nose was long and predatory.

"Come in, Mr. —" the banker shot a hasty glance at the card upon his roll-top desk, "Lockridge." His voice was as colorless as his features.

"Delighted to meet you, sir!" boomed Sam, advancing with outstretched arm. He seized the banker's reluctant hand and pumped it vigorously.

Horrman shot a quick glance from beneath his eyebrows, "I understand you bought Bubbling Spring?"

Sam waved airily, "A mere nothing! Merely a little side bet while I look into more important matters."

"Such as?" prompted the other.

The pseudo Cyrus K. Lockridge smiled and winked knowingly, "At this stage, my dear sir, those matters must remain confidential. Suffice to say that I represent important Chicago interests and that developments, surprising developments, are foreshadowed in this valley."

"A railroad!" murmured the banker, "And Bubbling Spring blocks the Gap!" His small, shrewd eyes dwelt upon his visitor with puzzled interrogation, "How did you persuade Harrigan to sell?"

"The power of the dollar," replied Sam portentously.

The strings tightened around Horrman's thin lips, "You are aware, I suppose, that this man is an escaped convict, now under arrest for another murder. Money won't help him much in Yuma — if he escapes hanging."

Sam leaned forward, his voice dropped to a low, confidential tone, "As one business man to another, Horrman, I suggest that we should not be too precipitate. I confess I am amicably disposed towards the young man — he saved my life in Tucson. There are also some legal details to be smoothed out before the transfer is completed." The palms of his hands came together and slid softly to and fro, "Where millions are involved, a few choice crumbs fall from the table, eh? You and I can work together, Justus — to our mutual advantage."

Horrman eyed him shrewdly, "A share in Bubbling Spring?"

"Possibly — very possibly!" Sam straightened and moved towards the door. "Think it over — Justus!"

No sooner had he breezed out when the banker tinkled a cowbell on his desk. The clerk hurried in.

"What did he bank, Pollard?"

"A thousand, but I swear, Mr. Horrman, he had another fifty thousand in his roll — it was big enough to choke a horse."

For the third time that morning, Harrigan's cell door gritted open upon sandy hinges. Limpy thrust his head inside, "Light a shuck!" he rasped without preamble.

"Figure you can't make it stick, eh?" taunted the prisoner, gathering himself off the bench. "Some day I'll get the rights of Harry Hartstone's killing, too."

"Vamoose!" repeated the deputy without interest.

"How much," he inquired abruptly, as Harrigan gathered up his belongings in the office, "did thet city slicker pay f'r Bubbling Spring?"

"Not a damned dollar," mocked the rider. "I signed it over to him f'r free, jest to beat a certain bloodsucker in Vulture Valley." With that he slammed on his Stetson and left.

He was drifting along the plankwalk towards the livery barn when the scent of fresh-baked pies pulled him up short before the steamy window of Swanson's old restaurant. Puzzled, he glanced up at the façade, he could have sworn the place had been closed these five years or more.

A crude, freshly painted sign spelled out, "JUST GOOD PIES."

He pushed aside hanging fly-curtains and stepped in. A row of frayed stools were set along a newly varnished counter. Through an aperture in the rear partition a matronly woman was visible, bending over an iron cookstove. Back towards him, a buxom brown-haired girl was filling a large coffee urn. "No more pies today," she flung over her shoulder, "They're all spoken for."

Harrigan's jaw slackened with surprise. In the dark he would have sworn it was Ruby.

When she turned around he grabbed the counter for support. It was Ruby, queen of The Double Eagle, but a new Ruby, light-brown hair neatly braided and pinned around her head; face innocent of paint and powder; a white apron pinned over her plain gingham dress.

"Well, if it isn't the bad man from Yuma!" She smiled, and her eyes were mocking, as of old. Resting her elbows on the counter, she looked him over. "How's the side?"

"As good as new," he grinned. "I could sure swallow a slice of pie and cup of cawfee."

She walked back to the kitchen, returning with a sizzling apple pie upon a plate. She drew a mug of coffee, cut the pie in quarters and set the whole before him.

"Heard they brought you in for Chunky's killing?" she commented.

"They did, but this gent eased me out." He laid Sam's card on the counter.

"Reads like he's a big potato."

"He is!" Harrigan dug into the pie.

"And I gamble he wants your land."

"He's got it!"

"There's one born every minute," she said shortly and watched him eat without further questions.

Harrigan pushed away the empty plate with a sigh of satisfaction. "Never tasted better!" he declared and dropped a dollar on the counter.

Ruby pushed it back, "This one's on the house!"

He fished out the makin's, "How come you changed your job?"

"Shirtsleeves to shirtsleeves in one generation! Me, I go from slops to silks and then back in less."

"So you quit the saloon!"

"By request."

"For why?"

Her lips curled in a cynical smile, "Whitey didn't approve of my associates."

"Meaning me!"

Ruby raised her shoulders. They were shapely even beneath the gingham, noted Harrigan.

"How come you opened this dump up agen?"

"I'll have you know this is no dump," she flared, "and I sell every pie we can bake." Her voice dropped, "There's deep currents in this town, Yuma. Sometimes I think it's like a sleeping rattlesnake. That's why I'm sticking around — I just can't tear myself away before it rattles and strikes."

"Cut the deck deeper," he frowned.

She spoke slowly, tantalizingly, "Maybe it's just as well if we let lay."

"Does it tie in with Harry Hartstone's killing?"

She nodded, "Chunky, too."

"F'r Gawd's sake, Ruby, quit this sunfishing!" His voice was harsh with feeling, "Jest what do you know?"

"Not enough to talk — yet."

"Hell, you're gonna talk!" His fingers fastened upon her wrist, dug deep into the soft flesh. "Who plugged Harry?"

With a quick twist she wrenched her wrist free, gazed tight-lipped at the red weals that marked the imprint of his fingers.

"Wal?" he demanded tightly.

"Yuma!" Her voice was suddenly tired, "Do you want me to be found with a hole in my back — like Chunky?"

"What loco talk is that?" he asked angrily.

"If you don't —" Her composure melted, anger blazed in her dark eyes and she stamped her feet in a sudden surge of passion, "Damn you, Yuma, why can't you leave me alone? Beat it! Do you hear? Go to the devil for all I care!"

CHAPTER TEN

THAT EVENING the ACC bunkhouse buzzed like a beehive and the air was thick with speculation as to reasons for the arrest of Yuma, their new foreman. In the ranch house, a puzzled and unhappy Dude considered his new perplexity over Scotch-and-sodas that seemed to have lost their savor.

An excited yell from a lounging waddy brought the crew boiling out of the bunkhouse — to see the object of their debate calmly stepping down from his buckskin, while the missing black fretted on a hackamore.

"Gosh, Yuma, you're a sight for sore eyes," declared a sandy-haired, bowlegged waddy, as they bunched around him. He eyed the black, "You gun Chunky?"

"Nope!" said Harrigan shortly, lifting his saddle, "Some other gent beat me to it. He was found dead, shot in the back. Thet's why Limpy took me in."

Attracted by the commotion, the Dude stalked through the gloom. "By jove, if it isn't Yuma — the prodigal has returned!" he drawled, with manifest relief. Then he sighted the black and his voice thrilled with feeling, "Blackie!" With ill-concealed affection he ran his hands over the pony's sleek coat, fondled its silken muzzle. Harrigan could have sworn he glimpsed moisture in the Englishman's eyes.

"Two of you fellers rub them hawses down," he directed, "and feed 'em a measure of grain apiece." He turned towards the bunkhouse.

The Dude grabbed his arm, "You're coming along with me, old chap," he decreed, "and elucidate the mystery of today's happenings over a spot of whisky." Side by side, they walked across the yard. Harrigan was beginning to like the angular Dude, despite his glass eye. There couldn't be much wrong with a feller who thought that highly of a horse.

For days the routine of the ranch ran like a smooth machine. Busy with his job, Harrigan ceased to ponder upon the unexpected reappearance of Slick Sam, the perversity of Ruby and the strange undercurrents that he felt, rather than knew, pulsed through the valley. Then two punchers jogged in from their day's ride along the south line, agog with excitement. They reported that strange doings were afoot around Bubbling Spring. Men in high laced boots, packing queer contraptions mounted on tripods, like photographers, were peering around and planting white flags all over the country. They were camped by the spring with a spring wagon and two tents.

Early next morning, Harrigan rode over to investigate. As the waddies had reported, the terrain around his old homestead was crisscrossed with stakes, to which small white flags were tacked. Two young fellows in trim knee pants and high boots were setting out more.

The foreman headed for the chaparral by the spring, above which a lazy tendril of smoke coiled from a campfire. The rays of the rising sun gleamed white on the canvas bows of a wagon and the curved canvas of tents.

A burly form arose from beside the fire and greeted him with a hearty boom. It was Sam, garbed in gray shirt and laced boots, like the others.

"Howdy!" roared the confidence man, "The early bird catches the worm, but the worm should have shown more sense and stuck to his soogans. You are abroad early, brother!" Sam was in great good humor.

Harrigan stepped down, "What in hell's doing around here?"

"Merely a preliminary survey, brother." Sam rubbed his hands, "Great things are afoot!"

"Why wouldn't I run them jaspers off?" Harrigan nodded curtly in the direction of the surveyors.

Sam bit the tip off a cigar, ignited it with a blazing twig from the fire. "Have you forgotten, brother," he asked softly, "Bubbling Spring is mine."

"Thet ain't what the county records say."

Unperturbed, Sam gazed at the sky, " 'Do not cut down the tree that gives you shade,' " he intoned. His chin came down, "from the Arabian, brother, and wise counsel." Sorrowfully, he continued, "I opened the gates of Yuma for you, and I eased you out of a cell in Powwow. Is this gratitude — or must I jog your memory further?"

Harrigan remembered his promise in the cell, made hastily and without thought, "Get me out of this tight and the land is yours, for free." It hurt to lose Bubbling Spring. "I guess it's yours," he admitted reluctantly.

"I also gave my word," smiled Sam, "One half of the profits, brother, and I see the glint of gold! Step into the tent yonder; I have the deed prepared."

Had Harrigan lingered he would have seen a livery rig, hauled by two tired plugs, toiling over the bumpy, faint-marked wagon road from Powwow. Grasping the lines was Justus Horrman. He, too, had heard of the white flags blooming on the plain below Buzzard Gap. He, too, was curious.

Sam met the rig as the ponies came to a grateful halt in the yard.

"Welcome, my dear Justus!" he boomed. "Welcome to the future flower of the prairie, the fair city of Buzzard Gap!"

Horrman slipped off a linen duster, shook it, folded it carefully and laid it on the seat. This done, he stepped down and looked around with noncommittal eyes. "City!" he commented tartly, "Of what — prairie dogs?"

" 'Where there is no vision the people perish!' The old prophets spoke truly, Justus!" came back the other sonorously. He slipped a hand beneath the banker's arm, steered him towards the nearer tent, "I have something more tangible inside."

Inside the tent, a blanket had been spread over several upended boxes, forming a table. On this, Sam unfolded a large map. Upon the crackling parchment a town was delineated, block upon block. Through its center curved a double railroad track. Around the depot, squares and rectangles were neatly tagged "Stores" — "Warehouses" — "Stockyards." There were even a bank and a theater. Across the top of the map, with many curlicues, the words, "City of Buzzard Gap," were inscribed.

"An idle dream!" snapped Horrman, but his sharp eyes missed nothing.

" 'The wise are prone to doubt,' " agreed Sam, unruffled. "From the Greek, Justus! But I have another map here, a most confidential document. Its mate is locked in the vaults of the Chicago and Western Railroad. This, I must confess, was obtained by devious means, bribery is such a harsh term!"

He unrolled another map, heavier than the first and soiled by much handling. It was stamped, "Chicago & Western R.R. — Preliminary Survey."

"Here," intoned Sam, "we have the results of a survey undertaken at enormous expense for the directors of the C & W and intended for their eyes only. You will note," he traced a parallel black line with his forefinger, "that steel will traverse Vulture Valley, cross the Dragoons at Buzzard Gap and thence continue west, practically duplicating Western Pacific service to California. There's hot blood between those railroad giants, Justus, hot blood!"

Horrman's small teeth were gnawing at his underlip, "A survey is no indication of action."

Sam smiled indulgently. "You will note the portions of the map hatched in red." He indicated broad colored bands running intermittently on each side of the parallel black line. "That, my friend, is land I have optioned for myself and associates at a cost, I may reveal, of several hundred thousand dollars. Why do we risk our capital upon a mere survey? Because, my dear Justus, at a secret meeting of the C & W directorate, held in Chicago on February 15th — four months ago — a resolution was passed to float a ten million dollar bond issue to construct the line. Our informant sat in at that meeting and pocketed ten thousand dollars of our good money for the tip — it would have been cheap at a hundred thousand."

"Here," his finger plumped on Buzzard Gap, "I feel we — I — have a bonanza — a goodly sum from the railroad for right of way, it MUST go through the Gap, and a fortune disposing of business sites and residential lots. You note it is indicated as a division point!"

"What do you mean — we?" Horrman was staring fixedly at the map.

Sam stole a quick glance at his pinched features, noted the swelling veins beside his forehead, the twitching of a nerve in his throat, and decided he was practically hooked.

"I have almost decided," he returned blandly, "to allow you to participate in Buzzard Gap."

"Upon what terms?"

"Well," Sam reached out lazily and picked up a sheet of paper, upon which were columns of figures. "I anticipate cashing in upon Buzzard Gap — land, right of way, and so forth, to the extent of $300,000. Here is the breakdown." He handed the sheet to Horrman, "I'll let you in upon an equal basis for, say, $50,000."

"Hard cash?" The banker's voice was strained.

"Tush!" chided Sam, with amusement. "I don't need the dollars. I have too much dormant capital as it is. I had thought of a half interest in the Valley Bank."

"My bank!" almost screeched Horrman.

"Almost a gift," the other assured him soothingly, "And — as a sweetener — I'll throw in another thousand acres of ACC range, bordering the railroad, at my option price, $15 an acre. Why, man, speculators will fight for that land at $100 an acre — when the news leaks out!"

Horrman sat silent, twisting in an agony of indecision.

"Friend Justus," suggested Sam kindly, "Think it over — but think fast! I have no great wish to sell, but this would be snapped up in Chicago." He smiled apologetically, "We all have our weaknesses. I have always yearned to be associated with a small, sound country bank."

Reginald Edgington-Tailborne was sipping his evening whisky-and-soda when the Mexican servant brought in a card. After his master had scrutinized it carefully, he ushered in a blond, hawk-nosed man, with piercing eyes and an assured manner.

"Welcome to the ACC, Lockridge," drawled the Dude, adjusting his monocle. "The name is Edgington-Tailborne, Reginald Edgington-Tailborne." He indicated the bottle of Scotch, "Be seated and partake of our feeble hospitality. Another glass, Manuel!"

Sam took his whisky neat.

"And how are things in bally old Chicago?" inquired the Dude courteously.

"Roaring as usual, great city, Chicago!" responded his guest, a trifle abstractedly. A brilliant possibility had suddenly struck him — why not cut this scion of old England into the Buzzard Gap melon? His fertile mind was actively canvassing ways and means.

"Arn't you the johnny who has been sticking a lot of silly flags around Bubbling Spring?" continued the Dude brightly. "Yuma, my foreman, was looking them over."

Sam seized the opening, "Mr. Tailborne —"

"Edgington-Tailborne — hyphened," corrected his host gently.

The big man inclined his head gravely. "Mr. Edgington-Tailborne, you see there the beginning of an epoch, the birth of a city, the fruition, if I may say it, of my life's dreams." He paused to meet the Dude's entranced stare. Hastily, before the spell should be broken, he continued, "Those humble stakes mark the spot where great buildings will rise, where commerce will flow, where — who can say? — a magnificent county courthouse will be carved from the stone of these eternal mountains."

"Good heavens, man!" ejaculated his listener, "What on earth will support this — aw — thriving city?"

"Surely," Sam's smooth features reflected incredulous amazement that any intelligent man could be so ignorant, "you have heard of the prospective railroad?"

"Tut, tut!" chided Edgington-Tailborne, unabashed "Who would build a railroad through this infernal desert? I distinctly recall that when I dropped in on Uncle Ernest, on the maternal side, in Chicago, the old buffer stated that his line had made a survey and regarded the idea of expanding west of Amaha as entirely impracticable."

"And what might your Uncle Ernest's position be, sir?" inquired Sam suavely.

"Chairman of the Board, Chicago and Western Railroad."

A glass crashed on the adobe floor and tinkled into fragments. The Dude cut short his guest's apologies with upraised hand, "A mere nothing, old man. Manuel, another glass!"

Sam poured again and his hand was steady. "This is in strict confidence, Mr. Edgington-Tailborne. From the most impeccable sources I am informed that the Western Pacific is contemplating running a branch line through the valley and Buzzard Gap."

"Then the jolly old stockholders should enjoin them," retorted the Dude.

With an effort, Sam smiled, "A matter of opinion! But what really brought me here was to endeavor to acquire an interest in, say, a thousand acres of ACC range adjoining Bubbling Spring. Would a twenty-day option at five dollars an acre interest you, sir?"

The Dude stuffed his pipe bowl, regarding his visitor with something akin to amusement. "My dear fellow, as range land it's not worth a dollar an acre, but when your city becomes a reality! Well, old chap, a hundred dollars an acre would be cheap."

Sam breathed deep, his own sales talk had tripped him. But Sam had a resilient mind. "Mr. Edgington-Tailborne," he came back with dignity, "I am a man of vision, I see a railroad, smiling homesteads, smoking factories. It is, I admit, a dream — a fond dream. That thousand acres will be my donation to the community in the form of a public park. The money? A mere bagatelle! But I must not forget that I am a business man, too. Five thousand dollars is an ample contribution."

"So you are one of those bally philanthropic millionaires!" The Dude smoothed his smudge of mustache, "I think, old bean, we'll call it ten dollars an acre — or perhaps I should hold it!"

"It's a deal at ten dollars!" Sam delved into an inside pocket, "I have an option form right here! I will pay $10,000 cash within twenty days if I take up the option — as I shall." He produced a fat roll of currency, smiled whimsically, "If you insist, I could pay you now. Shall we say a ten-spot as a token payment — until the deal is consummated?"

"Anything that suits you, suits me, old top," returned the Dude indifferently, "Have another spot and tell me about the great city of Buzzard Gap."

"You will, of course, keep this matter in strict confidence," urged Sam, as he left later.

"My lips are sealed," the Dude assured him solemnly.

Clear of the ranch, Sam released a low whistle. "Chairman of the Board, C & W!" he murmured, " 'Speak not of stones to a fool lest he cast them at thy head,' " Then, to the nodding pony, "An admirable sentiment, from the French!"

The following morning, the Dude strolled from the house and approached his foreman. Harrigan stood by the corral gate. He was setting the crew to work for the day. This was always a lively interlude, riders swallowing dust in the corral as they dabbed ropes upon their circling mounts; ponies sticking their bills in the ground and bucking out of sheer devilment at feel of the saddle; an exuberant waddy occasionally releasing a shrill yippee.

"An affable gentleman called last night," confided the Dude, "Mr. Cyrus K. Lockridge, a jolly old millionaire. He is a man of vision. He told me so in amazing detail."

Harrigan said nothing until the last pair of riders had jingled out of the yard, but his thoughts were not pleasant. Knowing Sam, he suspected his schemes. The Limey would be a push-over for that astute gentleman. "He sell you some land?"

"Good gracious, no! Haven't we enough land already? I would like to look over that — er — projected city. He has excited my imagination."

"We could take a pasear over that aways." Harrigan's lips twitched, "I'll stick the postage stamp on Blackie."

"I prefer it to an armchair," came back the Dude stiffly. Sly reference to his slick English saddle always nettled him.

From a high bench above Bubbling Spring the pair rocked their saddles and eyed the valley outspread below. The chaparral around the spring was patched green on the plain. Dwarfed by distance, adobe, tents, wagon were plain through the crystal air. A surveyor was sighting through his instrument while a rod man held a slim shaft erect. Up and down the swales, countless rows of stakes were specked white. And a man was setting more.

"Incredible!" breathed the Dude. The exclamation held more admiration than wonder. It might well have been a tribute to a master. He turned to Harrigan, "Shall we ride through the Gap?"

Their ponies breasted the precipitous trail, toiled upwards to the Notch. Wreathed by talus dust, they traversed the gloomy corridor and again drew rein when a great arid bowl lay before them, simmering, subdued and lusterless, beneath the blazing sun — Alkali Valley.

Harrigan dropped a sharp oath.

"Anything wrong, old chap?" inquired his boss, squinting across the alkali-blotched expanse.

"Stinkers!"

The Dude followed his foreman's pointed finger. Far out and spaced wide, three bands of sheep were crawling across the valley.

"Oh, sheep!" exclaimed the Dude, "Frankly, my dear boy, I can't conceive of a more harmless creature."

"Not feed enough to fatten a grasshopper," grunted Harrigan, "I don't like it."

"Come, come! How can they possibly affect us?"

Harrigan braced himself, his employer's ignorance was sometimes a trial. "What would you do," he asked patiently, "ef you was herding sheep and you lacked feed and water, 'specially if the next valley had grass hock high and plenty springs?"

"Naturally, I'd drive my animated mutton chops into the land of milk and honey."

"Thet's jest what I'm scared them snoozers u'll do, down yonder — drive through the Gap into Vulture Valley. Then all hell will break loose."

"But you forget ranchers are grazing the entire valley, old top."

"Three-quarters of the Valley is government range, and sheepmen are stubborn cusses. There ain't a gallon of real sweet water in Alkali Valley. We got trouble on our hands, boss, big trouble."

Sight of the flocks in Alkali Valley brought another memory back to Harrigan, that of a suntanned girl with clear eyes, as cool as a mountain lake; long evenings beside crackling mesquite campfires; the protest in her eyes when he rode off on a trail of vengeance.

CHAPTER ELEVEN

Cyrus K. Lockridge, sometimes known as Slick Sam, was not unduly surprised when, a day later, his glasses focussed the paint-scarred livery buckboard, far off across the flats, bumping along the trail to Bubbling Spring. When it rolled into the yard, Justus Horrman, the banker, sat primly erect upon the seat. Methodical as always, he folded his linen duster, set it carefully beside him, laid his driving gloves upon the duster and stepped precisely down. No one would have guessed from a glance at his neatly shaved features, gray powdered from the trail, and carefully brushed suit, that he had spent the better part of the previous night pacing his bedroom in the high-fenced bungalow where he lived alone, while greed and caution battled in his mind. The thought that strangers should walk in and grab the vast profits from land speculation that would follow in the wake of a railroad, touched him to the raw. For years he had seen this coming and laid his plans, but those plans had gone awry. Now, if he failed to grasp opportunity, it was apparent his chance was gone — forever. Half interest in the bank! It was a bitter pill but he had steeled himself to swallow it.

"Well, well, brother Justus!" boomed Sam, "I perceive you have heard the news. Regrettable, very regrettable, but these things will out!"

"What news?" snapped the banker. Sam's booming voice, his overflowing self-confidence, his very physical size, everything about this bland outsider irritated the precise Horrman.

"Take a look at that!" invited Sam, pulling a folded periodical from his pocket.

Horrman's quick glance went over the title, *Commercial Review.* He noted it was published in Chicago. Then his eyes darted down to a pencil-marked item on the front page. Quickly, he read:

C & W EXPANSION RUMORS

Persistent rumors are floating around LaSalle Street that the Chicago & Western R.R. will shortly push its steel through to California, and that plans to issue $10,000,000 five per cent bonds, secured by rolling stock and equipment, have been made to finance the project. At present the Union Pacific enjoys a monopoly of the profitable West Coast and intermediate haul. It is well known that the C & W has long been anxious to provide competition, but construction costs, particularly through the Dragoon Mountains, offered a formidable barrier. It is claimed, however, that a feasible route has now been surveyed, crossing the Dragoons in the vicinity of Powwow, a small town in Arizona. Interesting developments are awaited.

"I gamble the sharks are heading West right now," chuckled Sam. "Jehoshaphat! Won't there be a rush to get on the band wagon!"

"You spoke of an additional option," queried Horrman guardedly.

Sam read the avidity gleaming deep in his eyes.

"To sweeten the pot — a thousand acres at $15 an acre," he agreed. "It still stands — Cyrus K. Lockridge is a man of his word! What is a paltry fifteen thousand! We'll be talking millions before the summer's out."

"The bank," continued Horrman, and there was a quiver in his voice as though he were parting with an only child, "the bank is a private institution, owned solely by myself. Should we form a partnership, each would be responsible for the other's liabilities, which is not satisfactory."

Sam smiled, "I can present a financial statement."

Horrman checked him with uplifted hand, "I propose we form a stock company to control the bank. It could be capitalized at, say, $100,000, and one thousand hundred-dollar shares issued. Each would hold five hundred shares."

"An excellent suggestion," approved the other, "We'll need a bigger bank, brother, when the railroad comes through! And about the option. I paid $15,000 cash to the ACC for that. Just make out a check for the same amount and I'll transfer the land to you."

Horrman nodded, a vision of the potential $100,000 profit in that thousand acres shining in his mind. "We'll take the stage into Apache City tomorrow," he suggested briskly, "and engage an attorney at law to prepare the necessary papers."

"You are a man after my own heart," declared Sam. Horrman winced as the big man slapped him heartily upon the back. "Everything should be clear and above board, that's the way Cyrus K. Lockridge does business. Stick around, there's a bottle in the tent."

Horrman shook his head decisively and reached for his duster, "Thank you, no. I am not addicted to the use of hard liquor and I rented the rig for a half-day only."

Sam chuckled deep in his throat as the banker laid his whip to the plugs and stirred them into reluctant motion. The fish was hooked. Now all that remained was to fry it carefully and serve to taste. As the rig pulled out, he crumpled up the periodical that Horrman had scanned so closely and dropped it into the dying campfire, which was a careless way to treat a unique document — the first and only issue of *The Commercial Review,* printed in a limited edition of one. Expensive, but Sam never did things by halves.

Outside the Powwow Hotel, Cyrus K. Lockridge lounged in a rocker, cigar between his lips, benevolently watching the sluggish life of the cow town flow by. It was sundown when Harrigan rode into town to pick up the mail and snatch a quick two-fingers in The Double Eagle.

At sight of the rider, the confidence man raised a beckoning hand. Harrigan pulled in to the tie rail, dismounted and dropped into a rocker beside Sam. "Ther's more stakes around Bubbling Spring than a dog has fleas," he drawled.

"Pin-points of progress, brother," returned Sam sonorously. He rose, "Perhaps you would convey a package to Mr. Edgington-hyphen-Tailborne? I have also something of interest to you in my room."

Harrigan followed him through the lobby with its double row of shabby leather rockers, along the worn carpet of a passage in the rear where bedrooms opened off on either side.

Sam led the way into his room, furnished with the conventional brass bedstead, washstand with china pitcher, and ciga-rette-branded bureau. Two leather grips and a small trunk were stacked in a corner.

Harrigan dropped onto a straight back chair and watched idly as Sam unstrapped a grip. Amazement leapt into the rider's eyes when the big man lifted out a thick wad of greenbacks. Sam whetted his thumb and rapidly flicked hundred-dollar bills onto the bureau top. When the crisp stack threatened to spill over on to the floor, he shook the bills together, snapped a band around them and tossed the wad carelessly to Harrigan, "With my compliments to friend Hyphen. Ten thousand dollars, brother, in full payment for a thousand acres."

Harrigan hefted the pack and stared at the currency incredulously, "You ain't paying $10,000 for a thousand acres of bare range?"

"I most certainly am, brother!" Sam smiled expansively, and added in a mellow tone, "I sold — for $15,000!" Again he flicked off bills, spilled a fistful into his visitor's lap — "Two-thousand-five hundred dollars, brother, one-half of the profit in accordance with our verbal agreement. This, I trust, is merely a preliminary dividend."

"Doggone it!" ejaculated Harrigan, "Ain't no one in this valley loco enough to pay fifteen dollars an acre for fifty-cent land."

"No one but Justus Horrman," smiled Sam.

"Horrman!" choked the other. He could say no more.

Sam snipped off the end of a fresh cigar, " 'Happy the man who hath not the defects of his qualities,' from the French, brother, meaning that friend Horrman is so dazzled by the sight of gold that his clear-sightedness is impaired. I might also quote Shakespeare, 'Men's faults do seldom to themselves appear!' "

"I guess you could sell cinders in hell," admitted the rider with wide-eyed admiration.

Sam beamed again. "These financial transactions," he cautioned urbanely, "should be regarded as strictly confidential. Faith, such faith as I have carefully nurtured in my associate, is a tender plant that may wither when exposed to the strong light of publicity."

"Associate?"

"Justus Horrman — we shall shortly become co-owners of The Valley Bank."

Harrigan straightened, stuffing the greenbacks into his pants pockets, "I gotta get outa here afore I go loco. Ther's talk Arizona will be a state before long and they'll elect a governor. I wouldn't be a mite surprised ef it was you."

Head still awhirl from the impact of Sam's financial transactions, he dropped into the saloon.

There was the usual sprinkling of patrons along the bar. The evening was young and the dance floor deserted. Two girls were drinking with a lone puncher. By the far wall the usual groups of card players were bunched around tables.

Harrigan took his drink slowly, speculating upon Justus Horrman's investment. So buried was he in thought that he failed to observe a redheaded rider break away from a group on the further side of the room and thread across the floor towards him.

The feel of a gun in the small of his back jerked him out of speculation into cold reality. His head came up. In the back-bar mirror he focussed Red's rugged features, unsmiling now and cold with contempt.

"Keep them paws on the bar," growled the rustler, "I should smash yore spine, you double-crossin' son." He lifted Harrigan's gun and stuck it beneath his waistband. "Now hit f'r the corner table. Git going!"

It was all done so quietly that not a head turned as the pair crunched across the saloon.

Outwardly unmoved, Harrigan mentally cursed his carelessness. Since the night the ACC crew had cleaned up the rustlers, Red had slipped out of his mind entirely. With the breakup of the gang, he figured the red-headed rider had pulled out of the valley.

Then he glimpsed the two men seated at the table towards which Red was herding him. One was a stranger, stamped hardcase all over. The other was the mixed-blood, Lerew the knifer, whom he had left in a Yuma cell.

"Meet Yuma, boys, the rattlesnake who sold out Colorado's gang!" Red's voice was harsh. "Take a gander at the sidewinder afore I gut-shoot him."

Recognition flashed into Lerew's beady eyes. "Hell ef it ain't Harrigan, who busted out with Slick!" He thrust Red's vacated chair out with a boot, "Rest yore laigs!"

Conscious of Red's ominous form bulking behind him, Harrigan dropped onto the chair.

"Slick still smearin' wisecracks around?" inquired the 'breed, pushing a part-filled whisky bottle and glass across the stained table top. There was no animosity in his voice. Chances were, thought Harrigan, hefting the bottle, doublecrossing was such a commonplace to him it meant nothing, or maybe he just wasn't interested in Red's troubles.

"Sam's riding his own trail," he replied. "We split at the gates."

Lerew smiled in bleak reminiscence, "There's a gent who kin spit in the eye of the devil — then borrow his roll."

Harrigan poured slowly, filling the dirty glass until it brimmed but Red had seen that trick before. His voice came from behind and above the prisoner, "I'm watchin', Yuma — and I gamble I kin feed you a lead pill faster'n you kin ditch thet rotgut."

"Set down!" said Harrigan with faint impatience, "I like to look a man in the eye when I talk to him."

"You couldn't look a coyote in the eye!" flung back Red, but he hooked up another chair and pushed in beside the man he had disarmed.

"Now get this!" Harrigan's voice was sharp edged, "I 'crossed nobody! I traded lead with Colorado and quit. I was hired by the ACC and I fought for the iron."

"Yuh tolled us onto ACC range," accused Red.

"Yep, like a string of jugheads following a bell mare," taunted Harrigan.

"Ain't thet double-crossin'?" bristled the redhead.

"F'r gosh sakes quit whittle whanging!" cut in Lerew impatiently. "I kin use you, Harrigan!"

"The handle's Yuma!" came back the other with plain disinterest.

"Lissen, Yuma!" The 'breed's voice lowered, "We been casin' the bank. It's a cinch! Jest a lunger behind the wicket and a two-bit manager. Red and me kin hist it with our arms tied. Jake here kin cover the gateway, but we gotta have a jasper tuh handle the hosses. You're it, Yuma — a quarter cut!"

"I ain't bankin' on him for no getaway," declared Red vehemently, "He sold me out oncet — and once is plenty."

"You gimme my gun and we'll shoot it out," brindled Harrigan.

"Bottle it!" barked Lerew. "You jaspers are as techy as teased snakes. Le's figger it this away: Jake handles the hosses, Red, u'll cover the getaway and me and you, Yuma, hists the bank."

Red growled agreement. The man called Jake nodded indifferently. Harrigan shook his head in violent dissent.

"I suppose you want tuh meet us out of town and collect your divvy?" demanded Lerew irately.

"I don't want nothing, I jest want out."

"You ketch religion?" The breed's voice was derisive.

"I'm riding a straight trail!"

Lerew roared, hammering the table with his clenched fist, "Git thet, fellers! He's sent up f'r murder, he conks a guard, he busts out of Yuma, and he sez he's riding a straight trail!" His beady eyes mocked Harrigan, "I guess they got a dodger out f'r you. Mebbe we should turn you over tuh the sheriff and collect — fust."

Harrigan shrugged.

"Mebbe we should plug him," offered Red, Harrigan's defection still rankling.

The prisoner became aware that Lerew was no longer staring at him, but past him, across his shoulder, and his gaze was fixed as though he was hypnotized. Wondering, he looked around and understood.

Standing at the bar, chatting with Whitey, the manager, was Sam, impressive in neatly pressed dark suit, white shirt and stiff-brimmed Stetson. Even at that distance the sparkling diamond pin in his flowing tie was plain.

"Say!" whispered Lerew, almost in awe, "Ain't thet Slick?"

"It sure don't look like Sam to me," came back Harrigan.

Ignoring him, the 'breed kicked back his chair, moved across the room. Harrigan half rose to follow, but Red's edged warning pulled him down.

From the corner table, he watched the 'breed's unkempt figure as he approached the immaculate Sam, untrimmed hair streaming lank beneath his shapeless Stetson, holster bumping against grease-stained pants, gray shirt stiff with dirt. He saw Sam break away from Whitey with a boisterous laugh, then turn and stroll beside the 'breed towards the corner table.

Cigar between his lips, Sam stood above the seated men, blandly looking them over, "Am I supposed to know these gentlemen, Lerew?"

"Harrigan, mebbe," the 'breed came back. "He got a black-top now and he's learned psalm singing." Sam's gaze fastened blankly upon the prisoner, "Well, well," he exclaimed jovially, "I do believe that is my young friend from the Snake Pen." He pulled up a chair, "This is quite a family reunion!"

"Lissen, Slick!" Lerew sank his voice, "We're framing a job — a big job — the bank!"

"Splendid!" beamed Sam. The cigar circled as he indicated nearby tables, packed with card players, "Don't you think it would be well to discuss this in more, er, appropriate surroundings?"

"Where would thet be?" inquired Red.

Sam gestured towards the stairway in the rear, "There is a gambling room upstairs. I will make the necessary arrangements. You gentlemen go right ahead!" Unhurriedly, he rose and sauntered back to the bar, while Lerew hit for the stairway, the others trailing him.

At the head of the stairs was a short passage, faintly illuminated by a lamp swung from the rafters. Doors were spaced along one side. Several opened at the clump of boots on the stairs and girls heads bobbed out.

Sam joined the waiting men. He inserted a key in the lock and swung open the first door. At a thought, he paused, "Would someone bring a little refreshment?"

A baby-faced, blonde, with golden curls and world-weary eyes, darted out of her room.

"Bourbon and glasses," smiled Sam and gave her a hundred-dollar bill, "The change is all yours, my dear!"

With a delighted shriek, she flew down the stairway.

Lerew scratched a match and set it to the wick of a lamp, hanging above a large circular poker table and covered with green baize. Comfortable chairs were set around it. This was where big-stake games were played.

Lerew poured while Red closed the door. Circling the table, the five men pulled up chairs, drank in silence.

Sam set down his glass. " 'Seest thou a man diligent in his business, he shall stand before kings.' " He beamed around the circle, *The Book of Proverbs!*"

"Still bible punchin'!" grinned Lerew.

"There is no better reading, brother. Now to your very commendable project, relieving the bank of surplus capital. Are your plans made?"

"Yep!" The 'breed detailed the arrangements. "But," he concluded, "Harrigan's buckin'."

Sam's eyebrows raised and he glanced interrogatively at the rider.

"I don't want no part of it," reiterated Harrigan.

"It's rope him in or close his trap — f'r keeps," cut in Lerew venomously. "The jasper knows too much tuh run around loose." An idea struck him, "Say, mebbe we could plant him, now we got you, Slick!"

"My name," came back Sam softly, "is Cyrus K. Lockridge — for the record! Now, if I'm in on this, I handle it. And," from nowhere a Colt seemed to leap into his right hand, "here's my warrant!" He eyed Harrigan impersonally, "Our young friend will do his part! Tomorrow must be the day; noon will be excellent. I chance to know that there is a considerable sum in the safe which will be placed on the afternoon stage. I think," he thoughtfully rubbed the side of his arced nose with a long forefinger, "I will toll the deputy sheriff away and join you gentlemen on the edge of town. Is that satisfactory?"

"Lissens good to me," said Lerew. "You should know how, Slick, you pulled off some big jobs. Say, I gamble you was figgerin' on grabbing thet coin on yore lonesome!"

Sam smiled, the depreciating smile of a modest man.

"My gun!" reminded Harrigan, looking straight at Red. The rustler hesitated, slid the weapon across the baize with ill-grace.

"Next time, I'm acoming smoking!" warned Harrigan, dropping the forty-five into his holster. Red grinned his satisfaction.

Sam held up a hand, "Let this be distinctly understood, gentlemen, personal feuds are to be shelved until we divide — our just reward. Business before pleasure!"

"Say," demanded Harrigan, when the others had filed out and he stood alone with Sam, "You got me tangled up worse than a calf in a barbed wire fence. Don't you own half thet bank?"

Sam smiled serenely, "Legally, my interest does not go into effect for at least ten days. Brother Horrman has ample funds from which, er, to make restitution. 'He who seizes the right moment is the right man,' as Goethe so admirably phrases it."

"Count me out!"

"That job is like taking candy from a child, brother."

"I ain't got a sweet tooth."

"And our, aw, associates will not forget — remember there is a reward upon your head!"

"I still want out."

Sam sighed, "You had best ride for the ranch, brother." Then, sharply, "You will not breathe a word of this!"

"I'm no double-crosser!"

"If I thought you were, brother," There was cold menace in Sam's smooth tones, "You would never leave this room — alive."

CHAPTER TWELVE

R ED WAS bellied up to the bar when Harrigan dropped down the stairway and dodged through the couples who were now whirling on the dance floor. The rustler was watching the stairway, too. When he caught Harrigan's eye he tapped his holster significantly.

Harrigan stepped close, eyes icing over, "Any time suits me, feller!"

"Thet goes double," grinned Red, "But Lerew sez to save yuh f'r the job. Meet in the alley, side of the bank, at noon." He sobered, "You duck out this time, Yuma, and I'll get yuh ef I have to trail yuh to hell."

Harrigan lifted his shoulders and moved away. Sooner or later, it was plain, the discord that lay between them would have to be erased by gunsmoke. It was too bad about Red, he mused. Lawbreaker though he was, the rustler was as straight as an arrow, according to his lights.

He picked up the ACC mail at the post office wicket in McArdle's Store and pulled out of town, jogging along the wagon road that skirted Gunsmoke Creek. Sullen clouds blacked out the moon and darkened the plain, and dark forebodings rode with the lonely horseman. He was damned if he showed up in Powwow on the morrow and joined the gang — and he was damned if he rode clear of the holdup. He had no doubt but that the bank robbery would be carried through as slick as glass, a job like that was child's play to Sam. But if he took part, he would bear the renegade brand as long as he lived.

If he stayed out of the picture Lerew wouldn't forget, either. A letter to the sheriff would send him back to Yuma. Limpy might hold his hand for obscure reasons of his own, but he'd have no choice when orders came from Apache City. Red, too, had made his intentions plain, and he wasn't peddling talk.

There was no way out, except — and the brooding rider's nerves tautened at the thought — to 'cross the gang. A word to Justus Horrman would smash the scheme. He could keep out of the whole affair, send a waddy into town at sunup with an unsigned warning. Horrman was resourceful, he bossed Powwow. He would set a trap and clean the whole gang up. It was that — or Yuma.

A surge of self-loathing swept the notion out of his mind. Red had saved his life once. Sam was a square shooter, according to his notions. He couldn't play the cards that way, and have conscience brand him a double-crosser. The hand was dealt. Poor as it was, he'd play it, and play it straight.

When he stepped down at the ranch house, a voice came from the darkness of the gallery and Edgington-Tailborne's tall form was shadowed against the glow of a window as he rose languidly from a rocker.

"Thought you would be along, old top," he hailed. "I have been communing with the stars. A fellow can almost feel the quiet, doncher know. In these great silent spaces one is apt to dwell upon his youthful follies, misspent life and all that sort of rot. I don't wonder those whiskery old prospectors get bats in the belfry. Another hour out here alone and I verily believe I'd hear the bally angels sing. Any mail?"

Harrigan followed him into the living room and tossed the package of letters and newspapers upon the table. Then he dropped the thick wad of hundred-dollar bills beside it.

"By George!" exclaimed the Dude, "Did you rob the bank, by any chance?"

His foreman winced. "Nope," he replied shortly, "Thet city feller sent the dinero — ten thousand cartwheels. Seems he's paying for an option."

"Well, well!" chortled the Dude, "So he came through! Miracles will never cease. And I had him neatly catalogued as a mere bag of wind. Moneyed men do not ostentatiously display huge rolls of bills. I could have sworn that he was nothing more than an unscrupulous promoter, bent upon wheedling money out of the innocent populace. The city of Buzzard Gap! Did you ever hear of anything so fantastic? Which reminds me that I must drop a line to Uncle Ernest. These railroad moguls usually have an inkling of each other's plans. Now we must have a spot, old chap. Manuel!"

The Englishman was in a talkative mood, but Harrigan sat glum and silent — the cavern of darkness outside the windows reminded him of the Snake Pen that never saw the sun. He glanced down at his bronzed wrists; they were still scarred by the irons.

Powwow drowsed in the heat of midday. Everything living, down to the homeless curs panting beneath the plankwalks, sought shade. Even the canopied plankwalks were bare and, curiously, not a pony stood slack-hipped at the hitch rails.

The very quietude was oppressive. It held the tautness of the desert when storm clouds bank overhead and the very earth tightens with mounting tension as it awaits the clash of the storm gods.

Noisily, it seemed, two riders clattered down Main Street, one with a grin upon his lips. His Stetson was thrust carelessly back, revealing flaming red hair.

They wheeled into the lane that cut between the bank premises and the U.S. Barber Shop. One rider was already there, hunkered in the thin rim of shade afforded by the overhanging eaves of the bank building.

"Anything doin'?"

"Nope!" Jake, the hunkered rider, straightened lazily, "It's quieter'n boothill."

"Too damned quiet!" snapped Lerew with a trace of uneasiness.

"Mebbe thet slick hombre with a stickpin tolled 'em all out of town," chuckled Red. "Hey, ain't Yuma showed up?"

Neither man answered.

"The yeller, snake-gutted — !" swore the redhead. "I gamble he's hightailin' for the Border, scairt of his own shadow. Wal, thet makes it a four-way cut! We don't need no lookout, anyways. This is like snatching candy from a kid."

Lerew untied a gunny sack from his saddle-strings, rolled it tightly and stuck it beneath his belt. His fingers shook and he was as jumpy as a tin-canned dog. "Say!" he ejaculated suddenly, "Who piled thet lumber down the alley?"

Two heads swivelled. A loose stack of weathered two-by fours, remnants from some wrecked barn, blocked the lower end of the lane.

"Hell, thet's been dumped there f'r years," derided Red. "Le's get a wiggle on!"

"I don't like it!" declared Lerew, beady eyes slanting uneasily around, "It don't look right. You dead sure you seen it afore, Red?"

"Yep, Santa Claus left it!" grunted the redhead. His spurs jingled as he moved up the alley towards the street. Disquiet still in his eyes, Lerew hurried after him. Jake blew the dust from his six-gun, swung easily into leather, gathered up the hanging reins of the two riderless ponies and held them loosely. This was an old story to him.

The blued steel of a rifle barrel gleamed behind the lumber pile, but Jake was watching Main Street...a violent kick from within threw the swinging door of the Valley Bank wide open. Two men emerged at a clumsy run. Red, the first, hefted a six-gun. Behind him, Lerew packed a bulging gunny sack upon his left shoulder while his right hand lay on the butt of his holstered iron. As Red had foretold, it had been like taking candy from a kid.

On the wide wooden steps, Red grinned, swung around impulsively and threw a slug through the glass panel of the swinging door.

As though the shot was a signal, a leaden blast droned across Main Street. From the barricade of stacked flour in front of McArdle's Store, the doorway of Buskin's Saddle Shop, the flat roof of the hotel, the alley beside The Double Eagle, Winchesters barked and Sharps roared, spitting flame and thunder as their reports merged in savage chorus.

Red spun around like a top, the grin frozen upon his features. For a moment he stood swaying stupidly, then he was hammered down by pitiless lead. Lerew leapt forward like a maniac, twisting and dodging as he raced along the front of the bank. Bullets splintered the plankwalk at his feet, ricocheted with shrill protest off the rock-and-adobe bank, showered him with broken glass as windows were shattered above, but still his darting form was untouched. He doubled around the angle of the building, plunged into the alley and gained a brief respite from the scourging lead.

Three ponies milled restlessly in the narrow lane. Jake's limp form was sprawled in the dust.

Sucking air into his lungs in deep, panting gasps, the 'breed stumbled down the alley, grabbed the trailing reins of his chestnut gelding, leapt into leather, flinging the gunny sack across the horn.

The spang of a Winchester echoed between the walls on either side and fire spat from the lumber pile. The bullet buzzed over the renegade's shoulder. Dropping low, he spurred the chestnut viciously, herding the two remaining ponies before him towards the mouth of the alley.

Leaden hail again swept Main Street as the two riderless ponies broke from the alley. The first went down in a squealing dust flurry. The second, wild-eyed with fear, bolted down street. Behind it streaked Lerew, flattened upon the chestnut's withers, rowelling the maddened pony. Whining lead kicked spurts of dust between the gelding's drumming hooves and buzzed around the prone form of its rider like a swarm of maddened hornets, but Fate, ever capricious, decreed a miracle.

In seconds, the fugitive had pounded out of sight behind the dust churned up by his mount's flailing hooves — and with him went the loot.

Armed men boiled out upon the plankwalks. Sam, a Colt still smoking in his fist, stepped out from the doorway of the hotel, a harried-looking drummer behind him. Talk bubbled as eager citizens gathered around Red's bloodied remains and packed into the alley where Jake's distorted mask stared up at the sky.

Justus Horrman burst out of the bank, the hollow-cheeked clerk, face blanched, at his heels. Breathlessly, he broke into the group crowding Red's body, "The money! Where is it?"

"I reckon," opined a mustachioed oldtimer, "It's hell-bent for the Border."

A chuckle ran around the onlookers. Horrman was slightly less popular than the tax collector in Powwow. Lips locked, he jerked away, sighted the gaunt deputy limping across street with cradled Winchester. Kicking dust, he rushed to meet him.

"The currency! The gold!" he ejaculated.

"One jasper made it — and packed the loot," said Limpy laconically. "I'm gathering a posse."

"You allowed the miscreant to get away — with my money!" accused Horrman, "After Mr. Lockridge's warning!" His voice shrilled with anger, "It's inexcusable, it's — it's criminal!"

"Did I make the jasper bullet-proof?" demanded the deputy, with a touch of truculence. He shouldered past the fuming banker. Horrman stood alone in the middle of the street, hatless in the blazing sun, trembling with rage and frustration.

" 'The more the knave, the better luck,' " quoth Sam, striding up to the disconsolate banker. "Better move into the shade, Justus. Old Sol has a fiery breath."

"Gone!" muttered Horrman, moving mechanically towards the plankwalk. "Thirty thousand, if there's a dollar, and that fool deputy claimed they'd never get beyond the door."

"Fate's mighty aggravating at times, brother," boomed Sam, towering beside him. " 'He that is to die by the gallows may dance upon the river,' from the Italian!"

"To hell with your platitudes!" flared Horrman. Eyes wild, he scurried back into the bank.

Sam watched as the irate little man crunched over the broken glass that lay thick in the entrance, laughter lurking in his eyes.

Plagued by thought of the impending bank robbery, Harrigan fretted around the yard throughout the morning, unable to drag his thoughts away from the crime and its consequences. A dozen times he was tempted to send a warning to the banker, a dozen times he thrust the idea out of his mind. Little use as he had for the renegades, he could not bring himself to betray them, even though their deaths would erase, for awhile at least, the nightmare of return to Yuma.

Finally, when the strain became almost unbearable, he threw his saddle on the buckskin and headed blindly across the plain, not caring where he rode, his mind roiled by conflicting emotions.

As the sun dropped westward he found himself in the broken terrain below Buzzard Gap. Heedlessly, reins slack and his thoughts dwelling upon a knot of riders spurring for the Border, he drifted through the low hills, scabbed with dust-greyed mesquite.

Around the flank of a hill, a beady-eyed rider, with lank black hair and high cheek bones, rowelled a lathered chestnut.

Harrigan's gaze dwelt idly upon the stranger as the jaded chestnut labored along the trail towards him. Although the rider's features were yet no more than a faint blur beneath his sombrero, his carriage seemed vaguely familiar.

The flash of sunlight upon metal telegraphed a warning. Instinctively, Harrigan ducked low — and a slug sliced the air above the buckskin's ears. Alert now, Harrigan dove for cover, sliding his Winchester out of the boot. As he left the saddle, another shot speared from his assailant's gun. Before the stranger could throw down again he had squirmed behind the cover of a massive boulder.

"I'll be doggoned!" he muttered. He pulled off his hat and peered cautiously around the rock at ground level. There was nothing to be seen save a faint stain of blue powder smoke above the trail ahead and a riderless chestnut gelding standing with drooping head.

Still in the dark as to the motive for the attack, Harrigan lay slack — waiting for the stranger's next move. The shadows of the peaks began to grope with lengthening fingers across the valley. The distant, deep bellow of a bull rumbled into the hills and died. The buckskin's bit chain jingled as it nuzzled a lean clump of grama.

Slowly, as he lay belly-flat on the warm ground, anger began to build up in the rider's mind. Luck alone had saved him from the stranger's lead. Chances were the jasper was stalking him now. He'd need more than luck if he was to get out of this tight with a whole skin. It was a plain case of kill or be killed, and he didn't stomach being converted into buzzard bait.

With calculating eyes, he scrutinized his surroundings. The dips and rises of the terrain were plain marked by shadows cast by the sinking sun. On either side the ground sloped upward to low-lying ridges, with patched brush and littered rock that offered cover aplenty. A cautious man, he reflected, could skulk around and make his getaway when the sun dropped behind the Dragoons. But he felt no itch to leave — not until he had traded lead with the stranger.

A dozen paces behind him, the ground dipped and rounded boulders marked a long-dry watercourse. Again, Harrigan removed his Stetson, slid it sideways over the sandy earth until the crown projected ever so slightly beyond the smooth side of the boulder. A crash awoke the echoes. A slug screeched off the boulder.

He jerked the Stetson back with a humorless grin. Seemed like the hombre ahead was a mite jumpy. He had him placed now. Carefully, he set the Stetson so that it was barely visible on the further side of the boulder, then began to worm backwards, dragging his Winchester.

His feet dropped into the declivity of the watercourse. Pressed low, he eased his body down and took stock of his surroundings. He was lying in a narrow ditch, shallow and thick with skunkweed, that twisted obliquely up the ridge across the flank of his assailant.

The stench of the skunkweed was nauseating as his body crushed it, squirming steadily upwards between the boulders along the curving watercourse.

The ditch shallowed as it slanted upwards until the hatless, dust-plastered rider paused, twisted around for a look-see over the edge. He froze as a rattlesnake glided silently beneath a rock.

Down in the bowl, behind him now, the buckskin was still cropping peacefully. Immediately below, the sweated chestnut drifted aimlessly, but there was no other sign of life.

Head motionless, Harrigan searched the checkered patchwork of shadows that curved down and up the opposite ridge. His pulse quickened — one of the shadows had moved. With grim intensity, the rider watched and presently made out the vague outline of a man, inching forward, boulder to boulder, so slowly that his movements were scarcely perceptible.

Eyes hard as the rock around him, Harrigan cradled the Winchester against his shoulder, levelled it with careful deliberation, squeezed trigger. Before the sharp spang of the report had awakened the echoes, he levered and fired again, and again. The shadow no longer moved.

Rifle slanted forward, he slowly rose and dropped down the hillside. Cautiously, he approached the dark blob, stood above a gray-shirted rider lying upon his face, crooked fingers dug deep into the sandy soil. A rifle lay beside him. With mounting curiosity, he bent, grasped a shoulder and levered the body over — It was Lerew the 'breed.

With furrowed brow, Harrigan stared at the dead man's slack features. How come Lerew was riding towards the Dragoons — alone? Still pondering, he headed for the buckskin, swung into the saddle and gathered in the chestnut. Then he rode back to the dead man. It was then, at a hunch, he fingered the swollen gunny sack, tied behind the cantle of the chestnut's saddle.

With growing understanding, he fished out his Barlow knife and cut the sack free. Severing the thong wound tightly around its neck, he upended the sack and shook — a glittering cascade of loose gold and packets of wadded greenbacks showered upon the dusty ground.

Harrigan dropped upon his knees and, wondering, grasped a handful of the gold and watched it trickle through his fingers. So engrossed was he in his find that he did not hear the muffled thud of hooves behind him.

A girl's voice, clear and contemptuous, jerked him to his feet like a startled animal, "Killing seems to be a habit with you, Mr. Harrigan!"

He whirled around. Setting their ponies, were Joan Findley and her sheepman father.

CHAPTER THIRTEEN

THERE WAS no mistaking the condemnation in the eyes of the sheepman and his daughter. Standing beside the body of Lerew, with the loot heaped on the ground at his feet, Harrigan cast around frantically in his mind for an explanation that would dissolve their suspicions and knew he could find none. The evidence was too damning.

"Thet hombre, ma'am," he said evenly, "was making his getaway from a bank holdup."

"And you were checking the loot!" came back Joan Findley with cool mockery.

"Jest looking it over."

"For the bank, I assume!"

"Afore I tote it back to the bank."

"You always have the most plausible explanations!"

Harrigan was edgy after the gun duel, but he held his temper. "I'm packing the body and the dinero into Powwow right now," he declared, "Mebbe you folks would ride with me?"

"I feel safer — at a distance!" With this parting shot, Joan kneed her pony and wheeled away. Her father, sparing of speech as usual, said nothing as he reined after her. Harrigan stood motionless, watching as they walked their ponies uphill, topped the ridge and dipped down, out of sight.

He grasped the slack body in the middle, swung it across the chestnut's saddle, roped it securely in place. All the spirit had been rowelled out of the pony; it was too gaunt to buck. Then the rider pitched the coin and currency back into the gunny sack, thonged it to the horn and stepped up. With the chestnut on the lead, he headed for town.

Night had long shadowed Powwow when he jogged down Main Street, the chestnut dragging. Light from The Double Eagle and the hotel entrance spilled across the ruts. Then came the third shock of that fateful day — standing in the lobby of the hotel, plain in the yellow glow of the oil lamp suspended above, was Sam, unruffled as always, exchanging pleasantries with a drummer.

Shocked by surprise, Harrigan reined his pony to a halt. He had pictured Sam as either dead or splitting the breeze southward, where lay the Border. Speculation boiling in his mind, he wheeled to the hitch rail, tied his reins and stepped across the plankwalk.

Sam turned at sound of his spur-chains in the entrance, nodded, and continued to bandy talk.

Harrigan caught the big man's eye, gestured urgently. Sam broke away without haste and sauntered towards him.

"I got Lerew outside."

"Not alive!"

"Does it matter?"

There was no warmth in Sam's smile, "Lerew can hang us both!"

"Wal, he's dead!"

The big man's eyes thawed, "Excellent! Excellent! And the loot?"

"On my saddle horn."

" 'Let the miracle be wrought, though it be by the devil,' " quoth Sam. "From the Spanish, Hap!"

"How come you didn't light a shuck?"

"Action first, explanation later, brother!" Sam pulled at his long nose, gazing through the doorway at the indistinct outlines of the two ponies at the rail, one with a bulging load.

"I'm packing the body tuh the deputy," volunteered Harrigan.

" 'Impulse manages all things badly,' from the Latin," returned Sam absently. "We must conceal the body from prying eyes. Lady Luck will not smile forever," he murmured and moved purposefully toward the plankwalk.

Wondering, Harrigan followed.

Outside, Sam glanced keenly up and down the darkened street. Beyond the patient line of ponies, tied outside The Double Eagle and a drunk draped across the rail, there was little stirring. Apparently the chestnut with its gruesome load had so far escaped notice.

"Head north along the creek," directed Sam swiftly, "Pull rein a mile from town and await me."

"Say —" protested the thoroughly bewildered Harrigan.

"Debate destroys dispatch," cut in Sam crisply. "Do as I say. All shall be explained in due season."

Harrigan sat his saddle in the gloom beside Gunsmoke Creek and the willows drooped around him. The rider's mind was still awhirl as he endeavored to disentangle the events of the day. Nothing made sense — Lerew riding ACC range with the bank loot; the presence of Findley and his daughter in Vulture Valley; Sam's apparent immunity after staging a holdup.

A rider jogged down the faint trail that followed the creek. Harrigan whistled low and Sam, forking a livery hack, pulled towards him.

"Let us return yonder poor clay to the earth whence it came, brother." He swung to the ground, lifted down pick and shovel looped to the saddle horn. Without further ado, he stripped off coat and vest, rolled up the sleeves of his white shirt and commenced swinging the pick.

Wonderment deepening, Harrigan grabbed the shovel and threw the loosened earth aside. For a while they labored in silence, and a rectangular hole took shape.

"How did your trails cross, brother?" inquired Sam, panting with his exertions.

Harrigan told of his meeting with Lerew in the foothills of the Dragoons and the resultant gunfight. He paused to wipe the sweat off his brow and eye the deepening gash in the sandy earth. "Ain't this a mite long, the jasper ain't more'n six foot."

"We bury the saddle, too, brother," Sam continued to swing his pick with vigor.

"Maybe we should shoot the hawse on top of the grave, Indian style," suggested the rider with a touch of sarcasm.

"No, brother, the chestnut shall have its freedom."

"Ain't boothill good enough f'r this gent?"

"Where's the killing without the corpse?" came back Sam cryptically. He straightened with a deep breath, "You may unrope the body, brother."

Leaving the remains of Lerew in a nameless grave beneath the willows, with his saddle and bridle beside him, the two headed back to town. Harrigan dropped into a leather rocker in the lobby of the hotel and consumed impatient cigarettes while his companion returned the hack and tools to the livery. When the burly Sam at last reappeared, he grabbed the gunny sack and dogged him eagerly down the passage to his room.

Sam lit the oil lamp bracketed above the bureau and carefully pulled down the cracked window shade. Harrigan threw the gunny sack upon the bed and restlessly paced the worn strip of carpet.

"Maybe you'll enlighten me as to what all this sun-fishing is about," he suggested, an edge to his voice.

Sam dropped onto a chair, pulled out his cigar case and smiled serenely as he met the rider's frowning scrutiny.

"There is no mystery, brother. Lerew and his gang held up the bank at noon. His fellow renegades met their just fate. Lerew escaped with the help of the Devil. He headed south, swung around and hit for Buzzard Gap to elude the posse. His pony was played out. He met you and would have killed you for your horse." A stinker spluttered into fire and Sam applied it to his cigar. " 'Man blindly works the will of fate,' from the German!"

"How come you didn't beat it?"

Sam's eyebrows raised quizzically, "Is it possible, brother, that you would associate Cyrus K. Lockridge — co-owner of the bank, associate of reputable financiers, renowned city planner — with such ruffians?"

"You figured the deal and set the time."

Sam smiled with faint reproach. " 'Of evils we must choose the least,' from the Greek! When Lerew, our former cellmate, accosted me in The Double Eagle I faced a dilemma. To affront him would be to invite exposure, and I have had enough of Yuma. So I familiarized myself with his plans and it became easy to confute them."

"So you double-crossed the poor bustards!" said Harrigan slowly as understanding dawned.

"Let us rather say that I checkmated the unscrupulous and stood firmly on the side of the law," returned Sam, unruffled. "And, mark this, brother, I saved you from Yuma."

Harrigan scowled, "It don't set right!"

"Every man is the guardian of his own conscience," agreed Sam amiably. "Now let us consider the loot." He nodded at the bulging sack on the bed.

"Thet goes back to the bank!"

"Where else would it go, brother?"

Harrigan eyed Sam doubtfully; the big man's subtleties troubled him.

"In effect, you have already delivered the loot to the bank," continued Sam affably, "Seeing that I am the legal representative of the bank. By disposing of Lerew's remains we avoid embarrassing questions and you are in the clear. I shall return the loot in suitable manner."

"You swear Horrman u'll get his dinero back?" Doubt still stirred in the rider's mind.

"I give you my pledged word, brother, the loot shall be returned, but this calls for delicate handling." Sam rose and placed a kindly hand upon the troubled Harrigan's shoulder, "Who could handle it better than that sturdy citizen Cyrus K. Lockridge, the reincarnation of he who was once thief and robber?"

When the sound of Harrigan's spurs died down the passageway, Sam smiled benignantly at the sack of loot. " 'When good luck would enter,' " he murmured, " 'do not slam the door.' " Then, to the bureau, "From the Spanish!"

Bad news spreads faster than a fever. Before sundown the entire valley was discussing the holdup and looting of The Valley Bank.

When Sam, fortified by fried eggs and flapjacks, pushed aside the dusty fly-curtain of Jiggs Hash House the next morning, an uneasy crowd, all the more menacing because of its stony silence, had collected around the entrance of the bank.

By the time Pollard, the clerk, unlocked the door at nine o'clock a queue extended around the front of the bank, beneath the shattered windows. Immediately the door was opened, a flood of men and women — weathered ranchers, anxious clerks, bonnetted women, uneasy townsmen — flowed inside and jammed the premises. Another queue began to build at the door.

The run was on!

Sam stood in a corner, smoking his fat cigars and watching. On the floor, wedged tightly between his feet, was a fat leather satchel.

At ten o'clock the clerk eyed the press across the counter, then a bare cash drawer and nervously wiped his glasses. There wasn't any more! On shaking legs, he hurried into Horrman's office.

The banker stood by the window, now no more than a frame edged by jagged glass. His hair was neatly brushed, as always, and his shiny suit spotless, but there was a razor gash upon his sharp chin and lines around his mouth that had not been there before.

"Well?" he demanded, briskly.

"Our funds are exhausted, Mr. Horrman." Pollard dabbed at his forehead with a damp handkerchief. "There's still a crowd out there and they are in an ugly mood."

"Tell them I have sent to Apache City for more currency," snapped the banker. "They will be paid in full within two days — the jackasses!"

"I am afraid they won't wait." The clerk's voice was strained.

"They'll have to wait! Can I make money?"

"You — you tell them. I can't!" confessed Pollard shakily, and slumped upon a chair.

There had been little sound in the bank, save the shuffle of feet upon the plank floor and the mumble of muted talk. At the cashier's furtive withdrawal, fear ran over the throng. A whisper hissed through the elbowing, sweating depositors, "The bank's broke!"

Horrman's appearance was greeted with a rumble, deep-throated and menacing. He jerked out the clerk's high stool, mounted it and held his arms high for silence. Slowly the rumble died and an array of hostile eyes focussed his spare form.

"My friends!" He tried in vain to inject affability into his dry voice, "The Valley Bank is sound. I own the bank and I assure you that every dollar entrusted to us will be repaid —"

"Wal, cut the cackling and pay," shouted a whiskered rancher.

"Hear me out!" Horrman's terse face reflected no fear and his voice brittled. "Your funds earn interest. To earn interest they must be loaned. Your money is loaned out, upon ranches and upon cattle —"

"Yore a doggoned liar!" roared a beefy fellow. "Them renegades stole our dinero."

"I want my money!" a woman shrilled.

The voice of Horrman was lost in the clamor. What was before a close-packed crowd of sober citizens now became a shouting, shrieking mob, bereft of reason.

Sam, from his corner, eyed the banker's irate, gesticulating figure across the heads of the yelling throng and smiled.

A bullwhacker grasped the metal wicket with two brawny hands, wrenched it free and hurled it at Horrman; others scrambled up upon the counter.

Sam pulled his Colt, pointed it upward and thumbed.

The explosion reverberated like a thunderclap in the confined space … momentarily, it stilled the yammer. Heads swivelled. Attention concentrated upon the burly form of Cyrus K. Lockridge.

"Listen, friends!" Calm and commanding, he eyed the spread of angered, worried faces. "Wreck the bank and you receive nothing. Nothing! Have confidence, as I have, in Justus Horrman, and you will lose nothing." He bent, picked up the satchel and held it high, "Here are funds, my funds, sufficient to pay you all in full." He pushed forward, shouldering through the crush. "Wait, while I talk with friend Horrman!"

Inside the private office, Horrman eyed his saviour with anxious doubt. "It may require twenty, perhaps twenty-five thousand dollars to pay those people off," he jerked out.

Sam waved the satchel, "I have it here, brother. Funds from Chicago. Enough currency to satisfy those wolves outside."

"You will deposit twenty-five thousand dollars?" The banker strove to leash his eagerness.

"Deposit!" Sam eyed him reproachfully. "Deposit my associates' funds in a bank that cannot meet its obligations?"

"Don't talk like a fool, Lockridge! This bank is sound. In two days I'll have ample to pay all."

"Two days!" There was mockery in Sam's smooth tones, "In two hours they'll pull this bank apart and you with it, brother. Listen!"

Outside, the jam of depositors, packed more tightly each minute as new arrivals levered through the doorway, was growing restive again. Fists thudded on the office door.

"Get Leeman!" snapped Horrman to the clerk. "Tell him to swear in deputies immediately and restore order."

Sam smiled, "I understand he received an urgent call — out of town."

"Well, what's your proposition?" Dislike, disgust, disillusionment were mirrored in the banker's eyes.

"You have collateral?" inquired Sam blandly.

"Ample!"

"Mortgages?"

"Plenty — and well secured."

"I will take over $35,000 of your notes, secured by first liens on land and improvements, at a 25% discount, brother. And pay cash — here and now!"

Horrman's fists clenched and his face whitened with anger, "So you'd wring the last drop of blood out of me," he gritted. "And I took you as a partner!"

"When dollars come in the door, brother, friendship flies out of the window," returned Sam, unruffled.

A mighty clanging drowned the din outside. Pollard crossed the room and peered nervously through the keyhole. "The bank records!" he groaned, "They're pounding the safe door with a sledge hammer!"

"I have $25,000 — greenbacks," reminded Sam sonorously.

"Twenty per cent!" barked Horrman.

"Twenty-five per cent is the figure, brother."

"One hinge is off, the door's sagging," reported Pollard, with growing panic.

"Damn you for a Shylock!" choked Horrman, "twenty-five per cent!"

"And I take my choice of the bank's notes?" insisted his tormentor.

"Yes — yes — yes!" yelled Horrman, "Give me the currency while there is something left to save!"

Sam stepped unhurriedly up to the desk, unstrapped his satchel and shook packets of notes upon it. "Twenty-five thousand dollars in tens, twenties and hundreds," he stated. Then he strode to the door, "Hurry it out while I hold off the pack!" He smiled ironically, "I must protect my property. Ten days from date, I believe, one-half of what is left will legally be mine."

Panic is like a brush fire. It blazes up with lightning speed, rages feverishly and burns itself out as quickly as it begins. The run on the Valley Bank was born at 9 A.M. and died before noon.

Sight of stacked greenbacks, allied to Cyrus K. Lockridge's emphatic, though vague, assurances that he represented millions of eastern capital and those millions would guarantee that not one depositor would lose a single dollar, quieted the near riot. The cashier slowly, but steadily, paid out and the line shuffled at snail's pace past the wrecked wicket. Assured that their deposits were available if they wanted them, men began to tire of waiting and dropped out of the line. The stream grew to a trickle, and the queue shrivelled until it finally disappeared. By noon, there were more deposits than withdrawals, as those who had panicked earlier in the day decided their savings were safer in the bank than in their pants pockets.

Stripped down to vest and pants, Sam was shaving for the second time that day at the wash basin in his hotel room. He had to watch that black stubble on his upper lip; it didn't match a blond beard.

"Thirty-four thousand, four hundred in the kitty," he murmured as he lathered. "To which we must add six thousand, two hundred and fifty so generously contributed by brother Horrman — a neat little forty thousand dollars. Verily, this is a most productive valley!"

That evening, no one paid for drinks in The Double Eagle and Cyrus K. Lockridge showered gold with an abandon that brought delighted squeals from an attendant bevy of painted beauties. He was riding high.

At the bank, Justus Horrman surveyed the broken windows, the damaged safe and wrecked counter, and calculated his financial losses with misery in his heart. One ray of sunlight broke through the leaden pall of despair — he would recoup his losses, and more, when steel was laid in Vulture Valley.

In Chicago, a choleric, frock-coated gentleman was seated in the executive offices of the Chicago & Western Railroad. The frosted glass of the door panel bore the legend, "E. R. Rollins, Chairman of the Board." Before him, a yellow telegraph flimsy lay on the rich mahogany of a smooth flat-topped desk. Again he read the message: FANTASTIC RUMORS FLOATING AROUND REGARDING EXPANSION OF WESTERN PACIFIC THROUGH VULTURE VALLEY IN VICINITY OF POWWOW. OUR RANCH BORDERS PROJECTED LINE. PLEASE CONFIRM OR DENY. YOUR NEPHEW EDGINGTON-TAILBORNE.

The chairman of the board dabbed a stubby finger upon a button. A high-collared secretary hurried in. "Get me Jim Carson of the U.P. on the 'phone," spluttered Rollins, "and where the hell is Vulture Valley?"

There was no peace even at the ACC. The hungry crew was stampeding for the cook shack in response to the jangling call to supper when a puncher, as wild-eyed as his pony, spurred into the yard. "Woolies are floodin' through Buzzard Gap thick as doggoned locusts," he yelled.

CHAPTER FOURTEEN

C HUCK CALL was forgotten. Throwing questions, the crew bunched around the excited puncher's sweated pony, but he had little more to offer. Heading homeward after snaking a steer from a mudhole in Gunsmoke Creek, he had glanced towards the Gap — to observe with amazement that snow had fallen in midsummer. He was still staring, chewing upon the phenomenon, when he noticed that the snow patches were in motion. It was then he knew them for woolies and dug the hooks into his equally startled pony.

In a flash, thought of the Findleys came to Harrigan. The reason for their presence in Vulture Valley was plain now: they were looking the terrain over — the flocks he had sighted in Alkali Valley, the woolies pouring through the Gap, were the same — Findley sheep.

After supper, he broke the news to the Dude and found him only mildly interested. "Really, old chap," drawled Edgington Tailborne, "I fail to see that this has great significance. A few flocks of sheep would be lost upon these plains. After all, let us be reasonable: the world needs mutton chops as well as beef steaks."

"Boss," replied the foreman, with restrained impatience, " 'Member the rustler fracas? Wal, compared to what's brewing that warn't no more than a fist fight."

Harrigan was out of his bunk before dawn, saddling the buckskin by the light of a stable lantern. Sunrise found him on a high bench, gazing down into the bowl of the valley. Like a silver snake, Gunsmoke Creek coiled across the flats. Along its banks, great blotches of sheep showed dirty-white against the gray. On their flanks were quick-moving dots that were dogs, and surrounding them stumpy black sticks that were men. In the chaparral, smoke quavered upwards from a campfire and the bows of wagons glistened frostily.

Rising dust across the creek attracted his attention. He swung the glasses southward. Two riders were patrolling Turtle range. Further down the creek another pair stirred dust and further yet, a third pair. Bull Flint was primed for trouble, too.

No riders jingled out onto ACC range that morning. When Harrigan rode in, an atmosphere of taut expectancy pervaded the ranch. Trouble was in the air. Saddled and bridled ponies, the butts of Winchesters protruding from their saddle boots, were tied along the corral rail. Punchers moved restlessly around the yard, fretted by inaction. Another battle in the eternal war between sheep and cows was brewing.

Ignoring the questioning glances of eager waddies, Harrigan watered his pony, loosed cinches and lit out for the house.

Edgington-Tailborne was snugly ensconced in his favorite chair, sucking the stem of his briar, when the foreman reported, "Reckon they's a dozen or more herders and a swarm of woolies strung along the creek on our range. Them stinkers u'll spread like the plague."

"And what do you suggest, old fellow?"

Harrigan lifted his shoulders, "What kin we do but fight?"

"Come, come!" chided his boss. "Why be so belligerent? There is such a thing as compromise. From where I sit, a little diplomacy seems in order."

"Boss," said Harrigan, with the deep conviction of the born cattleman, "Ther's only one argument u'll convince a sheepherder — bullets!"

Hooves pounded outside and the two turned to the window. A cluster of riders swept past the house into the yard. Harrigan glimpsed four pack ponies on the lead, swollen sacks lashed to their kiacks.

One rider pulled off, a bull of a man on a sorrel stud. He reined up at the gallery, swung heavily down and clumped up the wooden steps. Without pausing or knocking, he pushed open the door and jingled into the living room. Flint hadn't changed a mite, thought Harrigan, with stirring resentment: he bulled over everyone and through everything.

The big cowman stood inside the door until his eyes adjusted to the muted light. Harrigan was tall, but the Turtle owner was taller, twice as broad and three times as heavy. Massive shoulders bulged under his gray shirt and his holstered six-gun looked like a toy against his heavy hip. His face was dark and seemed like weathered granite and his eyes, blunt as lava knobs, were sunk beneath bushy, graying brows.

He glimpsed the seated Dude and Harrigan standing silent at one side. "Afore you jaspers wake up," he grunted, "the snoozers u'll be spreading their soogans in yore bunkhouse."

"We are fully aware of the realities of the situation, old chap," said the Dude cheerily. He rose, carefully adjusted his monocle and eyed the visitor.

"My Gawd!" groaned Bull, "don't tell me you rod the ACC!"

"I exercise managerial functions, dear boy. The name is Edgington-Tailborne. This is my foreman, Yuma."

"Bull Flint!" came back the cowman briefly. His glance shifted to Harrigan. "Seems like I lamped you afore — somewheres. Ain't you the jasper who cleaned up on the brand-blotchers?"

Harrigan nodded curtly. "And hit you where it hurt," he thought.

"Wal, cain't you prod this wall-eyed gent into action? This ain't no time to squat."

"We were discussing the situation when you so courteously — walked in," volunteered the Dude, smiling. "Won't you, er, rest your body, Mr. Bull? Manuel!"

A rocker groaned as Flint eased into it.

He blinked as the white-coated Mexican appeared at his elbow with a bottle and glasses. "Never seed the like of it," he muttered, grabbing the whisky bottle.

He passed the bottle to Harrigan. "Packed a few sacks of salt-peter, had it stacked in the barn f'r months. Figgered we'd need it some time."

"Good heavens!" ejaculated the Dude, "Do we manufacture a special brand of gunpowder for use against these scoundrels who raise sheep?"

Bull's brow wrinkled. Harrigan grinned, "Thet's for the sheep, boss. Rank poison, but it don't harm cows."

"Indeed!" Edgington-Tailborne pulled out his tobacco pouch. "I suggest compromise, Mr. Bull. There is room for all in this great valley. Why poison the bally sheep and shoot the unfor-tunate herders when the whole matter can be settled amicably?"

Bull and Harrigan exchanged glances.

"Mister," said the cowman, "When rustlers grab steers we hang 'em; when snoozers grab range, we shoot 'em. How many waddies you got, Yuma?"

"A dozen."

"I brought eight. The rest of my boys are keepin' cases on the stinkers. Thet gives us twenty guns, plenty tuh clean up on the sons." He pushed to his feet, "Le's hump our tails!" Harrigan's eyes questioned his boss. The Dude nodded, doubt strong in his eyes, "You fellows are acquainted with the customs of the coun-try and I must bow to your decision. Frankly, I consider your action precipitate."

Twenty strong, a solid block of punchers jogged across the swales to repel invasion of Vulture Valley by the hated enemy — sheep. Ahead, Bull bulked upon his stud, and the Dude sat his smooth hunting saddle. Harrigan rode between them.

The green tracery of chaparral that marked the windings of Gunsmoke Creek lay like a verdant thread across the plain ahead. The sheepmen's light wagons became plain, the squat forms of herders, the swarming sheep. The yapping of dogs came sharply to their ears.

"Thicker'n maggots on a carcase," growled Bull.

Four men with black sombreros rode out to meet them. As they drew close, Harrigan recognized Findley. Tailing him were three younger men with weathered, unsmiling features, all cast in the same mould. His sons, guessed the foreman.

The advancing riders pulled down to a walk and Findley raised his right hand, palm open, in sign of peace. Bull checked the punchers and drifted ahead. Harrigan and the Dude stuck with him.

"We come in peace," said the bearded sheepman soberly.

"Then yuh can skeedaddle afore we bust up the peace," came back Bull roughly.

"Lack of water drove us out of Alkali Valley," continued the sheepman, "All we ask is graze until we can locate fresh range beyond the mountains."

"Ef them woolies ain't ambling through the Gap afore sundown," roared the cowman, "they won't need no water."

"We pack guns, too, mister," flung one of the younger men. Findley silenced him with an abrupt gesture.

"Give us two days!" he pleaded.

Bull eyed the sun. "Six hours!" he said shortly and wheeled away.

In the torrid heat of the bare plain, the punchers hunkered in the shadows of their ponies while their leaders talked, or more truly, Bull Flint talked. "I've a mind," he declared, "tuh hit the bustards right now, afore they get set. We kin drive the whole kit and caboodle into the creek afore you could shake a stick."

TOM WEST

Harrigan shook his head. "I tallied twelve herders at sunup, and they pack Winchesters. Ef we ride 'em down, they'll knock half our boys out of the saddle before we hit the woolies."

"Wal, do we set here on our hunkers like a bunch of tame Injuns waiting f'r a beef issue?" demanded Bull with faint patience.

"Nope, we hit 'em after sundown." Harrigan rolled a smoke, speculation in his eyes, "Lissen, I got an idea!"

"I still maintain we can compromise!" declared the Dude when the foreman had outlined his plan.

Bull ignored him, "You got savvy, Yuma," he declared, with approval. "I guess we'll hunt us some shade."

Peace lay like a benediction over the valley as the shadows thickened and a faint breeze rustled through the dry grass. Along Gunsmoke Creek the sheep clustered like swarming bees and a wisp of smoke marked a camp spot. But it was an uneasy peace. Beyond the flocks, dusky herders gripped their Winchesters and searched the deepening night. A girl in denims and rough flannel shirt tended the pots suspended over the fire. A bearded man paced slowly in and out of the flickering circle of light. Two younger men hunkered close by, cleaning their rifles.

The girl turned, gazed half-fearfully into the gloom, "Do you think they'll try and drive us out, Dad? You promised to leave, and they rode away."

"Think! I know." Findley's voice was bitter. "When did a cowman ever leave a sheepman in peace? There's a million acres of sheep range in these foothills, too poor for cows, government range — our range as much as theirs — and they'll fight to hold every foot of it!"

"Doggone hawgs!" commented one of the younger men.

"We kin fight, too," threw in the other.

"Fight!" barked their father. "What good does fighting do? Dead men, scattered flocks, more hatred!"

144

"Seems like we don't have much choice," came back his youngest son. He put the finishing licks on his Winchester, "I sure crave to get me that big hog of a cowman."

Out on the shrouded flats, a long line of punchers, strung in a wide arc, moved steadily ahead, hazing a dozen unbroken broncs towards the quiet creek. A six-gun blared and the line galvanized into frenzied motion. With yells and yippees, the punchers spurred their ponies. Terrorized by the uproar and the tingling cowbells hung around their necks, the broncs raced ahead, tails streaming and manes flying. Flame licked out of the darkness as the thin line of sheep guards threw down on the thundering horsemen. They had better chance to stop an avalanche. The racing punchers rode over and through them. Maddened broncs and yelling riders tore into the masses of fear-crazed, scurrying sheep; cut through and through the tight-packed bands of bleating forms, shoting and yelling, circling and swerving, in a delirium of noise and excitement.

From across the creek, rifles spanged and lead whined as Turtle punchers on the far side joined in the affray. But the shooting was not all on one side. Desperate herders, engulfed in whirlpools of terror-stricken sheep, dodging racing ponies and roaring six-guns, fought a grim, relentless battle in the flame-tipped gloom.

Harrigan, spurring his buckskin through a maelstrom of confusion, twisting and doubling, hazing gray-white bodies over the cutbanks of the creek, thought of Bull's words — they were like squirming maggots, and as plentiful. The incessant, terrified bleating of the harried sheep beat upon his ears, mingling with the frenzied barking of dogs, hoarse shouting of men, roaring of guns and, deadlier, the menacing drone of lead.

He glimpsed the lances of flame that stabbed through the darkness across Gunsmoke Creek and flinched involuntarily as a bullet buzzed by his ear. Turtle lead, flung blind, was no respecter of persons. The buckskin threshed out frantically as a dog fixed a rear hock and flung the animal off like a catapult. A gun-flash flicked almost beneath the plunging pony's muzzle and Harrigan whirled away, gunning the blurred form behind the flash…. A pallid dawn found a wearied bunch of punchers gathered in a draw two miles north of the creek. Beneath straggling scrub oak, jaded ponies stood droop-hipped, while their riders hunkered around, some with bloody bandages.

"Wal, we sure knocked hell out of the sidewinders!" Bull rolled a smoke and rested his bulk against a tree trunk, "I gamble thet creek's full of stinkers."

"They kicked us in the slats, too," commented Harrigan, "The ACC's got four empty saddles. You lose any?"

"Two," admitted the cowman.

"Six good men, f'r a mess of stinkers!"

"Wal, we served notice we don't stomach snoozers in Vulture Valley."

The Dude, heavy-eyed and unshaven, stifled a yawn. He was not used to losing sleep. "The whole affair was utterly senseless and ill-advised," he said testily.

"Button up!" growled Bull, irritably. He was bone-weary, too. "You can't tell skunks from house cats!"

"That may be so, my good man," the Dude's blue eyes frosted up, "Will you kindly inform me what we have gained? A polluted stream and six dead men, probably killed by our own guns — those fools were firing point-blank across the creek. Now those sheep herders are lining each side of the creek, which means another assault and more dead! I may not be able to distinguish skunks from house cats, but I find it equally difficult to distinguish you from a long-eared jackass!"

Harrigan blinked. This was fighting talk. He had never seen the amiable Dude angry before. His head swivelled towards the big cowman. Bull wasn't accustomed to back talk.

The Turtle owner's thick neck reddened, but he curbed his rising temper. He wasn't forgetting he still needed the help of ACC guns, considered the foreman.

"Hell, Limey, yore strange to this country — we gotta ace 'em out!"

Punchers began drifting around, attracted by the dispute. They circled the pair, eyes expressionless in sweat-smeared, fatigue-lined faces.

"The ACC is not sacrificing more lives to satisfy your senseless prejudice," Edgington-Tailborne's voice was taut. "I intend to ride to the creek, make a satisfactory compromise — and clear the Valley."

"Heck, boss!" cut in Harrigan, "There's blood in their eyes — they'll shoot you on sight."

"The jasper's got no more sense than a little kid with a big navel," growled Bull, with disgust.

"Kindly gather our crew," directed the Dude, shortly. Then to the cowman, "This is ACC range, Mr. Bull Flint, and I'll thank you to remove your person to your own side of the creek."

Fire sparked in the cowman's eyes. "B'gosh Limey," he blurted, "I've a mind to tear you apart, you cocky little rooster!" Big fists knotted, he moved heavily towards the Dude.

"Not while I carry this!" The Englishman's right hand dipped into a hip pocket and he pulled out a stubby derringer. "Another step, Bull — and I'll shoot!" He levelled the gun. Harrigan, eying his tight lips and set features, knew he meant it. Flint, too, sensed the Dude's determination. He hesitated, stopped, then turned away.

"Cinch up yore saddles, boys!" yelled Harrigan. "We're riding!"

With Edgington-Tailborne in the lead and Harrigan siding him, the bunch of ACC punchers moved across the flats as the rising sun painted the peaks. To their front, chaparral was green-veined along the creek. Beneath it, the earth was thick spotted with gray-white bodies. Around the riders, a small bunches of sheep were scattered across the plain, and two broncs, still belled, tossed their heads and high-tailed. Overhead, the buzzards were gathering.

A warning shot, sharp in the still air, whipcracked from beneath the willows. Almost spent, the bullet kicked up a small dust-devil in front of Harrigan's pony. He pulled rein, "Better halt that black boss," he warned, "They ain't fooling."

The Dude pulled out a creased handkerchief that once was white. "I am advancing under a flag of truce," he said stiffly, "You will remain here with the men."

"Maybe them snoozers ain't in a friendly mood," pointed out his foreman. "Tempers seem to be kinda tight all round."

But Edgington-Tailborne, disregarding, heeled his black and cantered ahead, the soiled handkerchief trailing from his upraised hand.

Another report echoed thinly from the creek. The upraised arm dropped and the Dude's body sagged.

With a quick oath, Harrigan spurred forward, waving back the punchers. He grabbed the headstall of the black and led it back, out of range. Edgington-Tailborne swayed in the saddle. Eager hands lifted him down.

Blood soaked his limp right arm. Harrigan slit the shirt sleeve. A neat hole was punched through the flesh, below the shoulder, and it was bleeding profusely. The foreman unknotted his bandanna and bound the wound tightly. Face bloodless, half-dead from fatigue and shock, the Dude tried to swing up into his saddle again and failed. "Give me a hand!" he gritted.

Harrigan boosted him into the saddle. He heeled the pony, heading again for the creek. The foreman ran after him, grasped a rein, swung the pony around. "You loco?" he ejaculated.

"Yuma, please remember that I give orders on the ACC!" The Dude's voice was faint but brittle. Harrigan's hand dropped away. Right arm hanging. Edgington-Tailborne heeled his pony and headed again for the willows.

"The gordamned stubborn mule!" muttered Harrigan, eyes searching the creek bank for another flash of fire.

"A gosh-durned salty gent," demurred a puncher gruffly.

CHAPTER FIFTEEN

TRAILED BY an elongated shadow, horse and rider plugged slowly across the sun-swept stretch of ground. Nine pairs of eyes followed their progress; nine men were tensed as they waited for another blast of lead to sweep the Dude's stringy form out of the saddle.

But no further gun flashes blossomed along the creek bed. With a sudden let-down of tension, the ACC punchers watched the Dude disappear beneath the willows.

They set themselves to wait for the Englishman's return. Harrigan began to sweat as the minutes stacked up. When half an hour had dragged past and there was no further sign of the Dude, the restiveness of the punchers threatened to explode into action. Harrigan held them back. He had heard no gun shot and, sheepherders though they were, he couldn't picture the Findleys murdering a man in cold blood.

A shrill yippee tore from the throat of a rider as the black pony again came into view. Harrigan could curb the excited waddies no longer. Whooping, they swept across the flat. The foreman spurred in their wake. If the snoozers got ringy now, he thought ruefully, the ACC would need a new crew. The sheepmen could pick them off like setting hens. The Dude was smiling, however, when the punchers circled him. The smile was a trifle wan, but it reflected triumph. A clean white bandage was wrapt around his wound and the arm bound across his chest. "Hostilities have ceased!" he announced. "Mr. Findley, who owns the sheep, will withdraw through the Gap and I have given my word that he will not be molested. I count upon you, Yuma, to show these people that we are, at least, honorable men."

The foreman nodded, pulling in beside him. "Someone did a nice job on your wing," he commented.

"A charming young woman insisted upon dressing it. Quite well spoken! She makes excellent coffee, too!" The Dude winced as his pony danced nervously around a dead sheep. "I think I shall return to the ranch, this infernal wound burns like thunder."

"You look like you're liable to topple out of thet slick saddle," said Harrigan, "and there ain't no leather to grab. Hey, Montana, you ride back with the boss! We'll chaperone the stinkers."

He pulled the punchers off. They watched the sheepmen gather the remnants of their flocks and steer them westward towards the Gap. It was sundown before the last band of sheep crawled upwards to the Notch.

Beneath the willows, a mound of loose earth, piled with rocks, marked the last resting place of those who would never again be troubled by sheep or cows. Across the darkening valley, a weary knot of riders headed back to the ranch.

The buzzards and coyotes left little, save whitening bones, to mark the scene of the fracas on Gunsmoke Creek. At the ACC there were fresh faces to replace those who lay forever beneath the willows. The Dude's arm was healing and the routine of the ranch rolled on.

The red Concord from the county seat brought the mail sack in on Thursdays, which gave Harrigan good reason to ride to town.

He tied his pony outside The Double Eagle, washed the dust out of his throat, pushed his Stetson back from his forehead and strolled leisurely along the plankwalk. Limpy was tacking a notice upon the front of a boarded-up store. The rider passed without greeting. He had little use for the gaunt lawman. To his mind, if Limpy had been smart, the deputy would have seen through the frame-up that sent him to Yuma. And how come he had allowed Ruby to bluff him in the shack? It just didn't add up right. Then the foreman's heart missed a beat and he hastily straightened his Stetson. Tripping along the plankwalk towards him was Joan Findley, trim in divided skirt and yellow silk shirt, a scarlet bandanna neatly knotted around her small neck and a stiff-brimmed Stetson set primly upon her curls.

"Howdy, ma'am!" he drawled. She stared straight ahead and he thought she was about to pass without deigning to notice him. But the girl stopped abruptly, swung to face him and tilted her head, "So you shot the bank robber to return the loot?" she challenged.

"Sure, ma'am!" he replied, mystified.

"And you hurried back to town with it directly we left you?"

"Jest ambled along."

"Then perhaps you can find a plausible explanation as to why that officer is distributing reward notices!" With this final shot, she tapped away.

Bewildered, Harrigan stared after her, then slowly retraced his footsteps to eye the notice newly tacked on the store front. With a deepening frown, he read:

$1,000 REWARD

Will be paid for information leading to the arrest of person (name unknown) who looted The Valley Bank, Powwow of $34,000 greenbacks and gold. Height about 6'. Black hair. High cheek bones. Probably a 'breed. A reward of 20% of all loot recovered will also be paid.

William Gotch, Sheriff,

Apache County.

Quick anger built up in the rider. A week back he had entrusted the bank loot to Sam, and Sam had sworn he would return it. It was plain that the confidence man had double-crossed the bank and made him — Harrigan — appear a thief and a liar. He was deep in Sam's debt, but this was too tough to chew. Eyes brittle with anger, he jerked down the notice, thrust it into a pants pocket and headed for the hotel.

The lobby was empty. Harrigan strode down the passage and rapped loudly on the door of Sam's room.

"One moment, friend!" boomed the familiar voice.

Fuming in the poorly lit passage, Harrigan heard rustling and sound of quick movement within. He was debating whether to turn the knob and burst in when the door opened. Sam, shirt open at the neck and minus tie, stood square in the doorway, blocking it, and something very close to annoyance glimmered in his deepset eyes.

"I am busy, brother," his smooth voice held a raw edge. "Perhaps you will return later?"

"Nope!" Harrigan bit off the word. Beyond the confidence man's broad form he glimpsed a woman. For a long moment they stood face to face, in a silent battle of wills. Sam turned, jerked his head.

Harrigan stepped back as a baby-faced blonde, with golden curls, slid out of the room and fluttered down the passageway.

"Now, my friend," there was no suavity about Sam now, "Kindly explain this unwelcome intrusion."

"Maybe you'll explain this!" growled Harrigan, and handed him the crumpled reward notice.

Sam smoothed it out, glanced quickly over it. "Believe not all you see or half you hear!" he murmured.

"Did Horrman get thet dinero?"

Without replying, Sam swung around, crossed the room and unstrapped one of his bags. Harrigan watched him, edgy with suspicion.

From the bag, the confidence man took a sheet of paper, handed it in silence to his visitor.

Harrigan read the thin, angular writing, "Received of Cyrus K. Lockridge the sum of $25,000 (currency.) Justus Horrman." It was dated the day after he had passed the loot to Sam.

"There was $34,000 in all," Sam's voice was restrained, reflecting the weary patience of a wronged man. "Of this, I withheld $9,000 — with Justus Horrman's consent. I explained that Wells, Fargo usually paid 25% for the return of bullion and he could do no less." He shrugged, "You know these bankers — 20% was all he'd agree to rebate." Again he dipped into the bag, came up with a thick wad of greenbacks. "I was holding this until I met you again, Hap. $6,000 — a small fortune! — I think that is a fair share of the reward."

Numb with surprise, the rider took the currency, "How come he's plastering these around?" he asked weakly, indicating the notice which Sam had dropped on the rumpled bed.

The other smiled, "Our friend has a devious mind; who knows what dark schemes may lie beneath it?" He placed a fatherly hand on the rider's shoulder, "Leave this to me, brother, and not a word outside. Put not your trust in princes — and bankers! Why would you worry, you have received your reward? 'The deed is everything, the glory naught,' Goethe, brother!"

Plagued with lingering doubt and a vague dissatisfaction, Harrigan left the hotel. True, he had seen Horrman's receipt for the bank loot and a liberal cut of the reward money bulged in his pants pockets, but how come the banker was running a bluff?

Cogitating, he wandered along the plankwalk until a slackness beneath the belt reminded him it was approaching noon and that he had swallowed no more than a quick mug of coffee before leaving the ranch. He dropped into Ruby's pie shop, eying her closely, remembrance of her previous outburst in mind. But she received him pleasantly.

"Long time no see!" she commented, dividing up a pie.

"I been busy." He slid upon a stool.

"Neat little filly you corralled across street!" Ruby was still engrossed in the pie.

"Yep!" he agreed, shortly.

"A good looker!"

He grunted.

"But not your type!"

"Say!" he burst out. "Quit poking your nose into my stall. You wouldn't know anything about the lady — she ain't your kind."

"Meaning a dance hall jane can't hold a candle to a genuine hundred per cent lady?"

"I reckon that sizes it up," he said roughly. "Now quit and gimme a slice of pie!"

She balanced the plate with the cut pie, danger signals flashing in her dark eyes, "I've a good mind to smear it over your ugly map. Since when has a sheepherder's daughter had class?"

"Wal, what's wrong with a sheepman's gal?"

"Nothing," mocked Ruby, "if she has a baby face and a wasp waist." She slid the pie across the counter and threw a fork beside it, "Here, guzzle your pie! You should be eating mutton chops!"

She patted her hair into place, "Some men would want more than a doll."

"Aw, button up!" he grunted. In silence, he demolished the pie.

Ruby drew a mug of coffee and wiped off the spotless counter. "Whitey," she remarked inconsequentially, "got a lousy record."

"What's it to me?"

"Shot a man in Abilene and welched on his debts in Omaha," she continued. "Then he got out of Cheyenne Wells two jumps ahead of a posse."

"How come you know so much about Whitey?" Harrigan pushed aside his empty mug and built a cigarette.

"I didn't wear ear muffs in The Double Eagle."

"Wal, it wouldn't faze me ef he was dodging a murder warrant," he returned with disinterest.

"Maybe that's what he should be doing."

"Say, what are you aiming at?" He began to sense some underlying meaning in her apparently aimless remarks.

"Droop-Eye, the swamper, could talk if he wasn't too scared to open his mouth."

"Talk about what?"

"Harry Hartstone's killing."

The rider suddenly tensed, his back straightened; he sat bolt upright on the stool, eyes fixed on the girl. All his indifference had fled now. "Jest what do you know about thet deal?" he asked tightly.

"Nothing, but Droop-Eye knows — plenty."

"Thet whisky-sodden old rat!"

"He was out in the alley when your pard was killed."

"You knew this right along!"

"I did not!" she declared vehemently, "and I'm a fool to talk now. Remember what happened to Chunky?"

Harrigan snatched his hat off the peg, "Where kin I find Droop-Eye?"

"He shacks up beyond the livery." Ruby's voice softened, "Go easy, Yuma, there's dynamite in that killing!"

But he was already beyond the fly curtains, striding down street towards the livery. At a thought, he dropped into the saloon and bought a quart of whisky.

Ruby's unexpected revelation roused a host of sleeping memories. Events of the past few weeks — the bank holdup, the sheepman's invasion of the valley, the demands of his new job — had crowded thoughts of his murdered partner into the recesses of his mind.

Now they rose like grisly specters to remind him that Harry Hartstone's killer still walked abroad, a free man, and that threat of return to Yuma would ever menace him until that killer was exposed.

The sagging livery barn lay at the south end of Main Street. Beyond it, the wagon road wound out on to the brushy flats.

There were few habitations on the fringe of town beyond an occasional board shack mouldering amid the mesquite or buried in the chaparral along the creek.

Bill Moggs, the liveryman, was stretched out on a pile of straw, back of the barn, snoring lustily. Harrigan nudged him into wakefulness with an impatient boot toe, "Droop-Eye, the saloon swamper, hang out around here?" he demanded.

"Down creek aways," muttered Moggs drowsily, "Now, f'r gosh sakes, beat it and let a man enjoy his siesta."

Harrigan paused before a tumble-down cabin, set beside the creek beneath a sun-blasted, storm-scarred old cottonwood. A torn blanket covered the glassless window and the door hung askew on broken hinges. A rusted hatchet was stuck in the chopping block and the ground was littered with broken bottles and empty cans.

Harrigan eased open the door and glanced inside. Light streamed through a hole in the roof. Mice scampered away from a chunk of mouldering cheese on a bench. Beside it stood an empty whisky bottle, two cans and a tin plate that held some hard biscuits. A blackened coffeepot stood on a cold stove in the corner. Blankets were heaped against the far wall.

Wrinkling his nose at the sour stench of whisky and stale food, the searcher was about to withdraw when the blankets heaved, and he saw that a man was bedded among them.

He quickly stepped across the dirt floor, bent, fumbled among the blankets, grabbed a thin shoulder and shook violently. The sleeping man moaned. Harrigan jerked the blankets away and hauled the befuddled swamper to his feet. Droop-Eye sagged against the wall, blinking uncertainly. A stained gray shirt and dirty pants clothed his emaciated form. Uncut hair curled over his ears and flopped across his forehead. Beard stubbled his jaw below hollow cheeks. A paroxysm of coughing racked him.

For a minute or more he stood gasping after the attack, then, "What d'ye want?" he wheezed.

Harrigan swept the bench clear, dropped down upon it and rolled a smoke, eying the derelict. "I want you," he said casually. "I come to kill you. Reckon you ain't got much to live for, anyways."

"Kill — me!" Droop-Eye gaped. His eyes sought the empty whisky bottle and his tongue lolled over caked lips.

"Take a shot!" invited Harrigan, pulling out the quart bottle, "You sure look like the frazzled end of a misspent night." The swamper grabbed the bottle with trembling fingers, twisted out the cork with yellowed teeth and tilted it eagerly.

Harrigan jerked it out of his hand and set it aside. "Guess you know why I'm agoing to rub you out, Droop-Eye?"

The human wreck, tottering against the wall, shook his head, dull eyes on the bottle.

"Because you killed Harry Hartstone, and I'm a pard of Harry's." He pulled out his gun and thumbed back the hammer.

The swamper continued to stare stupidly at the bottle. Droop-Eye's brain, decided the rider, was too pickled by alcohol to know what it was all about. He holstered the gun, stood up, slapped the shrunken, unshaven face sharply with his right hand. As the swamper reeled, he straightened him with a slap on the other cheek. Droop-Eye cowered, yelping. His tormentor gathered his loose shirt, shook him until it seemed his jerking head must snap off his shoulders. He threw him against the wall, slapped him again.

"I didn't kill Hartstone!" whimpered the swamper, weakly trying to parry the swinging blows.

"Who did?"

"Gimme a drink!"

Harrigan turned away and reached for the bottle ... A shoulder hit him in the small of the back. Off balance, he stumbled across the bench. It toppled and he went down, face first. Sprawled across the floor, he heard the quick pad of feet, caught a glimpse of a ragged form as Droop-Eye twisted through the doorway.

Cursing his carelessness, Harrigan scrambled to his feet and rushed outside. There was no sign of the swamper. He beat around in the brush, worked along the creek bank, searched the chaparral, without result. Finally, in disgust, he headed back to town.

Droop-Eye crawled out of a hole in the bank, below the cottonwood, glanced fearfully around, then slunk back into his shack. Cans, biscuits and mouldering cheese were spilled over the floor, but the bottle Harrigan had brought — three-quarters full — was set on the window ledge. Avidly, the swamper sucked it dry.

At sundown, Bill Moggs drifted down to The Double Eagle for his usual pick-me-up. Whitey, the manager, spelling off the barkeep, killed time with a game of solitaire on the bar. Moggs set a foot on the rail beside Limpy Leeman, who was nursing a short one. "Thet hombre Yuma was moseying around," he commented, for want of something better to say, "Looking f'r Droop-Eye. Now what in hell would he want with Droop-Eye?"

Limpy, impassively watching Whitey's play, ignored him. "Say," he told the manager, "You jest set a black ten on a black jack."

With no expression upon his pale features, Whitey picked up the ten and placed it carefully upon a red jack. Further down the bar, watching but saying nothing, was Bull Flint, drinking alone.

CHAPTER SIXTEEN

E HAD less chance of corraling Droop-Eye than of rounding up a jackrabbit, considered Harrigan, as he trudged along the creek. There were a thousand holes on the brushy flat into which a man might duck. Now that the rheumy-eyed swamper had eluded him he might just as well quit for the day.

Ruby's nose was flattened against the window of the pie shop as he rode past. He made a sweeping motion of his right hand to indicate failure and — in no cheerful mood — hit the wagon road north. He was halfway back to the ranch when he remembered the currency Sam had given him. Six thousand dollars was a trifle too much to pack around. His intention had been to bank the money in town, but Ruby's revelation and his abortive visit to Droop-Eye's shack had crowded thought of the reward money out of his mind. He was debating whether to turn back or ride on when recollection of the safe he had seen in the ranch office came to him. The money would be as safe there as anywhere.

"Kin I leave a little dinero with you?" he asked the Dude, when he delivered the mail.

"By all means, old chap," beamed Edgington-Tailborne.

Harrigan pulled the wad out of a pants pocket and dropped it on the table. "Six thousand," he said carelessly, "I got another thousand or two in my war bag I'll bring over later."

"Have you — er — inherited, or are these poker winnings?"

"Le's call 'em winnings," returned the foreman with a faint smile. "Say, boss, I'd like to drop into town again tomorrow."

"No objection at all, dear boy, all seems to be quiet — so far!"

Harrigan gave him a questioning glance, "You figuring on more trouble?"

"I would not be — too much surprised."

"Such as?"

But the Englishman would not be drawn out. "Let it pass," he said hastily. "We will cross our bridges when we reach them."

Before noon the following day, Harrigan was again in Powwow. He stepped down at the pie shop for a cup of coffee before seeking the bleary-eyed swamper again.

Ruby gasped when he brushed past the fly curtains. Her hands shook when she drew his coffee from the urn and it slopped as she set it on the counter.

"Say," he drawled, "you act like I was a spook. Either thet or you got a heavy hangover, I ain't sure which."

"Isn't it enough to give anyone the willies!" The girl shuddered, "Gee, Yuma, I can just feel them walking over my grave."

"Say, what's got inter you?"

"Don't tell me you haven't heard of the latest killing!"

"Nope, I jest drifted in." Cold premonition gripped him, "Not Droop-Eye?"

Ruby nodded somberly, "Yes — Droop-Eye! He was alive last night, they tell me, cadging drinks in The Double Eagle. Limpy found his body this morning. His head was smashed — with a hatchet. Limpy found that, too."

"Where?"

"In his shack. Bill Moggs was up there. He says it was awful, blood splattered over everything."

"What took Limpy up to the shack?"

"Don't ask me!" Ruby was on the edge of hysteria. Her voice took a shrill note, "First Chunky, now Droop-Eye, maybe I'll be next!"

"Quit squawking!" he said sharply, "Why would you be next?"

"Can't you see? Chunky was a witness of Hartstone's killing, and I swear Droop-Eye knew who the killer was. Now they're both dead! There's only Cheyenne left, and —"

"He's dead, too!"

Ruby eyed him open-mouthed, "How would you know?"

"I killed him!"

She shrank away, staring at him fearfully, "You, you didn't —"

"Nope, I didn't plug Chunky in the back, nor poleaxe Droop-Eye. Cheyenne pulled on me in Yuma and I beat the skunk to the drop." He sipped his coffee, brow creased, "I would say the gent who cut down Harry is getting a mite edgy. Ain't one hombre left who could tip his hand, except —" His speculative gaze dwelt on the girl, "You."

"Cross my heart, Yuma, I don't know nothing!" Ruby was almost weeping. "The girls in the saloon were always gabbing. One day, Madge, that's the blonde, said it was funny they didn't call Droop-Eye to the stand, because he couldn't have missed the shooting — They tossed him out in the alley just before Hartstone was killed. Gee!" she concluded miserably, "I wish I'd kept my fool mouth shut, my tongue always did wag too much!"

"I'd give my saddle," pondered Harrigan, "to know just why Limpy took a notion to leg up to Droop-Eye's cabin." He reached for his hat, paused, "You still living alone."

"Not any more!" Ruby was getting a grip on herself now and the old vigor rang in her voice. "I'm doubling up with Mrs. Wheeton, my cook, from now on. I'm packing a gun, too!"

The rider nodded approval. "Stick close to home after dark," he advised, "and ef you run into real trouble, grab a bronc and hit f'r the ACC."

The girl smiled with wry humor. "I can just see that fashion plate who bosses your spread receiving little Ruby with open arms!"

"The Dude ain't the only hombre on the ACC."

"Don't tell me you'd be glad to see me!"

" 'Member easing me out of a tight? Wal, I pay my debts!" He turned towards the door and did not see the disappointment that clouded her eyes.

Harrigan hesitated on the plankwalk. Now Droop-Eye was dead there seemed to be no point in sticking around town. But the odds were, he thought, that the jasper who smashed the life out of Droop-Eye either killed Harry Hartstone or knew who did. And that jasper was probably in Powwow.

A shadow fell across the scuffed planks. Harrigan looked up as the gaunt deputy limped past. His bleak gaze flicked over the rider without sign of recognition. Limpy's gaunt features held no more expression than a vulture's, considered Harrigan, and the lawman had just about as much heart. Who was to say that Droop-Eye was not alive when he visited the lonely cabin?

A wave of despondency swept over the rider. What chance had he of clearing his name now that the last witness had been silenced? His boots dragged as he crossed the street and pushed through the swinging gate of the saloon.

Bull Flint's big form barged through the batwings. He sighted Harrigan glooming over a heavy slug of bourbon. "How come yore swilling rotgut in Powwow" he bellowed, "when you oughta be kicking the pants off them snoozers?"

Harrigan straightened, lips tightening. Here was another of the black jacks in the dead man's hand fate had dealt him. "Last sight I had of the snoozers was when they were high-tailin' f'r the Gap," he said shortly.

"Wal, the bustards are back!" Bull tilted the bottle the barkeep slid towards him. "One of my boys lamped 'em at sundown yesterday. They swung north onto yore range." He snorted, "And thet damned Dood figgered he could talk 'em out of Vulture Valley! When I git through with the snoozers this trip they won't have any stinkers to take out!"

Harrigan set down his glass and pulled away from the bar. "Reckon I'll be needed out at the spread, Bull. You bringing your crew over?"

"Nope!" pronounced the Turtle owner emphatically, "I'm through with thet dangblasted Limejuicer. This time I handle matters my own way." He thrust out a beefy arm and checked the foreman, "How come yore riding f'r thet danged dood? He don't know sic-em!"

"He pays good!"

"So do I! I kin use you, Yuma. I like yore style. Ain't had a ramrod worth a damn since Chunky quit."

"Maybe later, Bull. Right now I reckon the Dood kin use me," stalled Harrigan. Would the Turtle boss be so eager to give him a job, he wondered, if he knew he was hiring Hap Harrigan?

He hit for his pony, loosened the reins and headed out of town. Woolies again! If it wasn't one brand of trouble it was another.

Another surprise awaited him when he rode up to the ranch house. Two ponies were tied at the rail and it needed but a glance at them to tell him who the visitors were — one was Joan Findley's bay mare and the other her father's claybank. He checked his pony, eying the animals with perplexity. Only one thing, he decided, could bring them to the ACC at a time like this — they were trying to make a deal ... As if any cowman in his right mind would make a deal with a sheepherder who had invaded his range! He wheeled away and rode around to the yard. Before he bulled in it might be a good idea to see if the crew could give him a line on just what had occurred since he left.

Something was wrong, very wrong. Harrigan sensed it as soon as he stepped through the bunkhouse doorway. The place was as quiet as boothill, the usual crossfire of cheery talk and good-natured badinage was absent. Punchers brooded around as silent and solemn as owls.

"What in hell's got into you jaspers?" demanded the foreman. "F'r gosh sakes perk up, you look as cross as a bunch of
snapping turtles."

"Stinkers are back!" blurted a waddy.

"Wal, since when did a mess of stinkers scare the daylights
out of yuh?" Thumbs hooked in his gunbelt, he surveyed their
sober faces, "Ef you gents don't stomach trouble you kin quit!"

"Thet's the trouble," put in another dolefully. "They ain't no
trouble."

Harrigan dropped onto a bench, eyed the subdued punchers
belligerently, "Someone cut the deck deeper," he snapped "I'm
jest a poor dumb saddle-walloper."

"Montana lamped the stinkers this a.m., heading f'r the hills,
along our west line," explained the first speaker, an older man.
"He humps his tail and brings the sad news tuh the boss. The boss
sez tuh lay off the woolies. It seems he don't see no reason why
steers and stinkers cain't lay down together, as friendly as two
kittens on a warm brick." The puncher moved a chaw of tobacco
and directed a brown stream beneath the table. "The boys was
hellbent tuh draw their time, but Montana sez to wait 'til we give
you the rights of it."

So that's why the Dude was expecting trouble, thought
Harrigan, and likewise why the Findleys were sitting cozy in
the house. He straightened, "I'm thanking you f'r the lowdown,
Alkali. You fellers set tight while I chew this over with the boss.
Maybe he needs to be set right."

The foreman had formed the habit of entering the ranch
house through the rear door, unannounced. But this time he
walked around to the front and rapped. He felt like a stranger,
heading in where he wasn't welcome.

The white-coated Manuel opened the door and stepped
aside, liquid eyes eloquent with surprise.

Harrigan's quick glance swept the room. The Dude, placidly
smoking, reclined in his favorite armchair. Close by and facing

him, sat Joan Findley. Grim-visaged, her father bulked by the rock fireplace.

"Hullo!" drawled the Dude, "arn't you getting a little ceremonious, old chap?" He rose, "This is Yuma, my foreman! Miss Findley and Mr. Findley, Yuma. Mr. Findley runs sheep."

"We have met Mr. — Yuma!" The girl's clear voice was curt. Her father's head jerked in almost imperceptible acknowledgement.

"Kin I have a word with you, boss?" inquired Harrigan, aware of the Findleys' cold hostility.

"About the sheep, I presume?" asked the Dude tolerantly.

His foreman nodded briefly.

"Later! Sit down and get better acquainted with our new neighbors!"

"I'll be in the bunkhouse — waiting!" came back the foreman unsmilingly. With that he swung on his heel and left the room.

Neighbors! he thought bitterly, as he rounded the house. There'll be hell to pay for this.

Not ready to face a flood of questions from the waiting waddies, he hunkered against the feed barn in the fading light and moodily rolled a smoke. It was dark and cigarette butts littered the ground around his feet when he finally heard the muted clip-clop of ponies' hooves and knew that the Findleys were leaving.

He lifted quickly and moved to the rear door, entered and jingled through the house.

Edgington-Tailborne was chewing a cold pipe with an abstracted frown when he walked into the spacious living room. "Er — take a seat!" ejaculated the Englishman absent-mindedly.

"He's bothered," thought Harrigan and dropped into a rocker.

"You wanted to see me?" There was unwonted formality in the Dude's voice.

"Yep!" Harrigan leaned forward, eying the other closely. "Get this straight, boss. You can't run stinkers and cows on the same range, and you can't run stinkers and hold a crew."

"You amaze me!"

"Hell, every jasper in the bunkhouse is pulling on the bit, ready to quit."

"In other words, this is an ultimatum!" came back the Englishman stiffly.

"Ef you mean it's a showdown — yep!"

The Dude slowly stuffed the bowl of his pipe. "First, let me make my position clear. I am not mixing sheep and cows. There's a wide stretch of semi-arid country beyond Dry Hills, which you have assured me is useless for range. However, it has some water and Mr. Findley avers it will support sheep. What remains of his flocks will be confined to that territory. The crew need never see them."

"Yep, but —"

"Hear me out!" broke in the Dude. "Sheep are profitable, far more profitable than cows in my opinion. My function is to manage this ranch at a profit. So far we have only seen red ink. Therefore, I have acquired an interest in the Findley flocks and am financially concerned in their well-being. Is everything clear?"

Harrigan nodded, his disgust plain. "You can't get away with this, boss!" he protested.

"Why not? Surely I can run whatever type of animal I wish on my own range?"

"Not in Vulture Valley!" came back the foreman grimly.

Edgington-Tailborne held a match to his pipe. "Does Mr. Flint consult me as to what policy he shall follow in running the Turtle?"

"You don't see this right, boss," pointed out Harrigan resignedly. "Cowmen don't cotton to nesters; they don't like rustlers, but they hate snoozers worse than Apaches."

"A most ridiculous attitude!"

The foreman rose. It was plain that argument was useless, "I guess I'm through."

"Perhaps that would be advisable." The Dude jumped up with alacrity, "I will get your — winnings." He emphasized "winnings." How come, wondered the foreman, the Englishman had turned so hostile. He had never acted this way before. Then, in a flash, the reason became plain. The Findleys had surprised him with Lerew's loot, kneeling beside the dead bank robber. They had been talking. The Dude had him branded as a killer and a thief. When Edgington-Tailborne stepped into the room again, Harrigan half opened his mouth to explain, closed his jaw with a snap — to hell with the ACC!

The Englishman set the wad of greenbacks on the table, thumbed some loose bills off his own roll and dropped them on the pack, "I think that squares the account, old boy!" He eyed the foreman with a measure of his former friendliness, "We may not see eye to eye, er, ethically, but you have done a top-hole job on the ACC, Yuma." A rueful smile hung around his lips, "Where will I find another such foreman?"

"You won't need a foreman, boss, because you won't have a crew." Harrigan pocketed the bills. "A puncher u'll swallow most anything, he'll spill blood f'r the iron, but he can't stomach the stink of sheep."

The foreman stepped into an atmosphere of expectancy in the bunkhouse. No one spoke until he hauled the soogans off his bunk and commenced to spool them.

"You quittin', Yuma?" He looked up, to meet Montana's worried frown.

"Yep!"

"So the boss ain't runnin' off the woolies?"

"I wouldn't know," said Harrigan shortly, tightening the rope around his roll.

"Heck, it's as plain as the horn on a saddle," growled another waddy. "Yuma don't want no truck with stinkers, and thet goes f'r me!"

"Me neither!" averred another. "Hell, le's all quit!"

A rumbling growl of approval greeted his words. There was a shuffle of feet and rustle of canvas as men hauled out their rolls. Harrigan's voice cut through the confusion, "Lissen, you mavericks! Ther's no call for a stampede jest because I'm pulling out. The boss ain't running sheep on ACC range — He's set the Dry Hills as a deadline. I gotta hunch, anyways, the woolies won't last long in Vulture Valley. Stick around awhile! The ACC feeds good and pays good. Maybe I'll be back."

The commotion stilled. Punchers paused in their packing, eyed him uncertainly.

"Kin we bank on thet?" Montana was the spokesman and Montana was their leader. Harrigan knew that the rest of the crew would follow him like a lead steer. He knew, too, that the Dude would be helpless if the ranch was stripped of its crew, and he'd never hire another as long as his range was tainted. Damn the mule-headed Limejuicer, thought the foreman, what would it take to make him realize that sight of a wooly affected a puncher just like a red rag did a bull? Aloud, he urged, "Hold your hawses! Hash it over with the boss at sunup. Ef you quit, he'll figure I tolled you away."

Montana threw his soogans back onto the bunk, "Sure, ef that's the way you want it, Yuma."

"I wouldn't want it no other way," responded the foreman. He shouldered his roll, "So-long, boys!"

"Wal, we're on the loose again," he told the buckskin whimsically as it jogged beneath the stars. "Me, they call me Sudden Harrigan — I was framed sudden; I quit Yuma sudden; I pulled out of Colorado's gang sudden and now I break away from the ACC sudden. And I gotta hunch the Dude's facing plenty trouble — awful sudden."

Two hours later he loosened cinches at a line cabin east of Smooth Water and turned the pony into the pole corral in its rear. He hefted his roll, picked a spot beneath a piñon and thumped the ground for rattlesnakes. For awhile, he hunkered beside the spooled roll, considering his next move. Bull Flint's offer came to mind. Why not throw in with Bull, he mused. If the granite-faced cowman was back of Harry Hartstone's killing there was no better place to get the lowdown than on his own spread.

CHAPTER SEVENTEEN

B ULL FLINT's spread was just about as uninviting as its owner's blunt features, thought Harrigan, as his pony plugged
across the glaring flats and the Turtle's buildings undulated on
the plain ahead through waves of heated air. Drawing closer, he
eyed the long, low adobe that provided sleeping quarters for Flint
and his crew. One end was blocked off, he remembered. This the
cowman used for office and sleeping quarters, while the balance
of the building, one long narrow room was lined with bunks and
housed the crew.

Smoke curled from the stovepipe chimney of a lean-to built
against the gray adobe, where the cook was busy at his endless
tasks. Parallel, stood a flat-roofed barn. A stretch of hoof-pocked
ground, that served as yard, lay between. Beyond were blacksmith shop, open-side wagon shed and other outbuildings, all
rock-and-adobe, sun-cured and colorless. Behind the bunkhouse
were the corral and pens. Above all, two windmills towered on
spidery legs, their blades motionless, while the water in the tanks
below shone like burnished copper.

Dust lay deep in the yard, fogging around the rider.

At a hitch rail that ran along the side of the adobe half a dozen
or more tied ponies flicked lazily at the flies. Harrigan wheeled to
pull in beside them and blinked when he read the brands — Lazy
H, Slash, Tumbling K, Rocking T, Boxed E — seemed like all
the ranchers in the Valley were gathered at Bull's for a meeting.
The rider's lips twitched; one thing was sure, it wasn't a prayer
meeting.

He stepped down, tied the buckskin and plodded through the powdery dust towards the closed door of Flint's office. Voices rumbled inside, a rumble that was abruptly chopped off when he pushed open the door and stepped across the threshold.

Bull's combination office and living quarters was jammed with the owners of the hitched ponies outside. Most every cowman in the Valley was hunkered around the walls or squatting on the bed, considered Harrigan, as his glance ran around the room. The air was laced with blue tobacco smoke, through which Bull bulked like a weathered image of a big Buddha as he sat atop his battered desk. There was no friendliness in the eyes that swivelled towards the visitor. He didn't need three guesses to know what they were discussing. His lips twisted, "Sorry, gents, I didn't aim to butt into a private augurin' match."

"We sure don't crave an ACC rep. at this roundup," bellowed Bull.

"I done quit the ACC," came back Harrigan and sensed a let-down in the tension.

"You showed good sense, Yuma," approved the Turtle boss. "Stick around. You'll want in on this."

Harrigan closed the door and leaned against it, debating which was the more disagreeable: the dust outside or the choking tobacco smoke that clouded the stuffy room. Bull gave his attention to the assembled cowmen. "We chewed this over plenty," he boomed. "Le's quit coyoting and get down to business. The snoozers slunk through the Gap agen and are runnin' their stinkers on ACC range. My boys been keepin' cases on 'em. Thet fool dood figgered he could talk 'em out of the Valley and they jumped right back. They's only one argument a snoozer understands — lead. Le's clean 'em out f'r keeps — with lead!"

A growl of approval ran around the room.

"Mebbe," said stolid Chris Hanson of the Lazy H, "Yuma would know how the ACC feels about this?"

"The crew feels your way, but the boss ain't hostile," came back Harrigan promptly.

"How come the owners welcome sheepmen?"

"The Dude, who runs the ranch, jest ain't acquainted with the customs of the country. To him, beef and mutton are both meat, and he ain't particular as to what brand of meat is raised on ACC range."

Bull's deep voice again boomed through the room, "Wal, it's agreed we clean up! You gents meet here two days from now with every spare waddy you got. Pack Winchesters and plenty chuck. This trip we ain't pushing no snoozers back through the Gap — We'll feed the bustards lead. They'll make good buzzard bait."

From dawn until dark the second day, punchers poured into the Turtle. Never had there been such a gathering of armed men in the Valley as far back as Harrigan could remember. Bull Flint wasn't overly popular; he'd trodden on too many toes. But invasion by the common enemy — sheep — brought the ranchers together as nothing else could.

Nothing in Apache County could stop this force, reflected Harrigan, eying the crowded yard. There were forty or more armed punchers hunkered around and new contingents were still drifting in. The cook was driven almost crazy trying to fill their stomachs, ponies packed the yard and saddles were stacked thicker than the flies in Jiggs' Hash House.

Twinges of regret troubled the newly made foreman of the Turtle when he thought of the lonely Dude. If the Englishman hadn't been so mule-headed he wouldn't have tangled with this trouble. Now he'd have to learn — the hard way. The Findleys were out of luck, too. If they stuck in Alkali Valley their sheep starved; when they strayed into Vulture Valley they were shot. He made a mental note to warn the punchers that there was a girl in the sheep camp. He would be in hell if Joan Findley stopped a stray slug. One thing was sure, nothing could save the sheep and

TOM WEST

the herders now. Even a sheriff's posse would be brushed aside like a pesky fly when the army of punchers killing time around the spread went into action.

They rode at dawn, a long procession that stretched like a loosely linked chain across the flats, still grayed with the clinging shades of night. Ahead jogged the cowmen, a solid bunch of sober-faced men, Bull Flint on his sorrel stud prominent among them. Then the Turtle contingent, eighteen armed men. Behind, riders from spreads as far distant as the Dos Cabezas, each bunched around its ramrod.

At Bubbling Spring they paused to water the ponies, rock saddles and snatch a quick smoke in the shade of the chaparral. By noon they were nearing the Dry Hills, squatting low on the plain ahead, heat-seared and sullen.

Like a huge diamondback, the array coiled through the hills, dust-wreathed and sweated. Higher and higher the ponies toiled until the leaders emerged on a bench, topmost of several that sloped, like a giant's stairway, down to a great dun plain below, a scarred waste of salt brush and mesquite that lapped to the barren flanks of the Dragoons.

But what drew every eye was a great band of sheep, every animal plain through the clear air, drifting like a white cloud across the flats, not two miles distant.

The leaders drew together in confab, while the punchers stepped down, tightened cinches and looked over their hardware. There was no attempt at concealment; no force existed in the Valley that could stand up against this strength. This was no raid; it was a clean-up, a lesson to sheepmen to keep out of Vulture Valley forever.

Harrigan rocked his saddle and idly eyed the flock below — peacefully browsing sheep, ever circled by restless dogs, herders drifting in their wake.

Something was wrong with the picture and he groped in his mind to place it. Realization came with the impact of a bullet — The sheepherders were not scared. It was scarcely possible that they could have failed to sight the big force of punchers spread over the bench above them. And it was unbelievable they did not realize that in a matter of minutes the punchers would swoop down upon them, scatter the sheep and cut them down. Yet they were acting as though there was not an enemy within a hundred miles. It didn't make sense.

Impulsively, he pulled his six-gun and loosed a shot. The gun seemed to boom like a cannon in the brooding heat. Startled heads jerked in his direction and Bull Flint broke out of the group of cowmen, charging towards him with fire in his eyes.

"What's got inter yuh?" he roared. "You gone crazy from the heat?"

But Harrigan's attention was on the sheepherders. As though they were stone deaf, they ignored the shot, although the echoes of the report were still reverberating through the hills. He saw one herder glance up at the bench and then calmly turn away. They couldn't be blind, too!

Bull was atop of him now, bellowing.

"Say!" he told the cowman curtly, "get a load of them herders!"

Taken aback, the Turtle boss stared down at the sheep, then pivoted to face his foreman again, "Wal?" he demanded wrathfully.

"We're bunched up here as plain as plowed ground. We act hostile, and they set down there as calm as toads in the sun. There's something almighty queer about this, Bull!"

Understanding dawned in the cowman's eyes. Puzzled, he again surveyed the grazing sheep. Punchers who had crowded around caught the sense of Harrigan's remarks and eyed their quarry uncertainly.

"Doggonit!" muttered Bull. "Like you say, it don't make sense. How would you account f'r it, Yuma?"

"I'd say it was a trap," came back his foreman promptly. "Else why would they stick around to be wiped out?"

"Trap!" echoed lank Bill Rogers, the Slash boss. He indicated the plain with a sweep of his arm, empty save for the flock. "How in heck kin they trap us? There ain't more'n four hombres down yonder and we tally seventy, mebbe eighty."

Harrigan lifted his shoulders, "Wal, ther's one sure way to find out."

"Rush the sidewinders!" roared Bull. "You said it, Yuma! Le's go!"

Spreading out as they dropped down the benches, the punchers urged their mounts forward. Loose rock abounded and checked the pace as the ponies slipped and slid on the steep grade. Harrigan reined back. His gaze swept the valley from side to side ... and his yell brought the scattered punchers to a startled halt. Following the direction of his pointed finger, they saw a cavalcade of U.S. cavalrymen, stiff as ramrods in the saddle, emerge from a draw on their left flank. Two by two, they deployed on to the plain. As the astounded punchers watched, the cavalrymen broke into a trot, a canter, thrusting a wedge between the sheep and their attackers. In the rear of the soldiers, Harrigan recognized Edgington-Tailborne on his black.

Bewildered by this unexpected development, the punchers milled around, uncertain whether to halt or continue their advance. Bull, as usual, barged ahead. The foreman chuckled silently as he spurred after his boss. Who would have figured the Dude packing this ace in the hole?

The troopers wheeled midway between the flock and the punchers, strung out into line and halted, facing the disorganized attackers.

A lieutenant pulled away and trotted forward at an angle to intercept the enraged Turtle owner. He was trim and clean-shaved, little more than a youth, but he represented authority, and he sat his saddle as though he was fully aware of it.

"This fracas ain't none of yore business!" yelled Bull, reining down his sorrel at the lieutenant's stirrup.

"Whose business would it be when armed riders make an unprovoked attack upon defenseless sheepmen?" inquired the shavetail politely.

"They got no right on our range!"

The lieutenant turned to the Dude, who had cantered up, "I understood this was your range?"

Cowmen and their riders were bunching around now, eager to see the outcome of this unexpected intervention.

"My range, or, more correctly, ACC range. It extends to those hills, old boy." The Dude indicated the benches down which the punchers had just ridden. "Actually, this is government range. This valley has never been grazed. There is not enough grass to support stock."

The lieutenant eyed Bull unsmilingly, "Then may I ask why you have led a force of armed men here?"

"Tuh run the snoozers off!" blustered the cowman.

"In other words, you defy the United States Government?"

"We got a right to clean varmints off our range."

"This," corrected the lieutenant patiently, "is U.S. Government range."

"Ours by usage!" threw in the Rocking T boss.

"My dear fellow," corrected the Dude, "this is ACC range, if anyone's, and I have given permission to the sheepmen to use it."

"They got no right in the Valley," boomed Bull.

"I could arrest you and other leaders of this armed force," said the lieutenant with cool casualness, "take you to Fort Apache and deliver you in due course to the civil authorities for trial. The U.S. Government has thrown this range open to everyone, which includes sheepmen, and it will protect their lives and property."

Fuming, Bull glanced past him at the gauntleted troopers. There were not more than a dozen. "I've a notion," he growled, "tuh clean up on you and the snoozers too."

"Then," came back the youthful lieutenant imperturbably, "you would have two squadrons to clean up at Fort Apache. And, after them, the entire U.S. Army. If your punchers kill one sheepman, Flint, now or later, you'll be hung for murder, and every man with you will stand trial as an accessory." With that, he wheeled his pony and rode back to the waiting troopers. The Dude tailed him.

Almost choking with frustration, Bull cursed the Army, the Dude and the sheepmen with equal impartiality. But the fighting spirit had oozed out of his followers. Even as his sizzling epithets scorched the air, they were covertly watching the silent, straight-backed cavalrymen and digesting the young lieutenant's words. It was one thing to buck a tolerant sheriff who had one eye on the next election, and quite another to dig spurs into the U.S. Government.

By unspoken agreement the crowd of riders began to slowly disintegrate. Cautious Chris Hansen was the first to beat up the benches with his Lazy H bunch. Others trailed him. In blocks, nodding ponies toiled back into the hills — the Rocking T, Tumbling K, Boxed E — until only the Turtle crew remained. Eying Bull's granite features, Harrigan knew that, even then, the tough old moseyhorn was tempted to rally his riders and sweep down on the hated sheep. At that, considered the foreman, they outnumbered the soldiers almost two to one. But there was something subtly menacing about those still-faced troopers, fencing off the gray-white flock beyond like a row of graven images. As a fighting force the Turtle might wipe them out, but they were more than a dozen armed men, they were a symbol of the power that lay behind them. The beardless lieutenant might be younger than any puncher on the crew, but he spoke with the voice of Uncle Sam.

Bull gloomed at the waiting troopers, "as sullen as a sore haided dog" as one of the punchers expressed it in the bunkhouse later. Then, without further word, he heeled the sorrel and neckreined it towards the hills. The Turtle ponies breasted the slopes in the wake of the other outfits, of whose presence nothing remained but vagrant dust drifting across the benches. As he dropped in behind his boss, Harrigan felt the chill of destiny. Sheep were in Vulture Valley to stay.

CHAPTER EIGHTEEN

Percival Pollard, cashier of the Valley Bank, was perched upon his high stool with an unbroken package of $20 bills in his hand and a puzzled look in his eyes. He set the pack upon his open ledger and commenced to systematically empty the cash drawer, examining the wrappings and edges of every package of new bills with minute care. Finally, the drawer emptied, he wadded his handkerchief and carefully wiped it out. This done, he inspected the handkerchief. The white fabric had gathered nothing but dust. Visibly at a loss, he gazed first at the handkerchief, then at the package of bills that still lay upon the ledger. It was incredible. It just did not make sense, but the fact could not be ignored — he had irrefutable proof that those bills were stolen in the recent holdup. Yet he had taken the package out of the cash drawer only a few minutes before!

He replaced the contents of the drawer, closed it, picked up the mysterious package of bills and stepped into Justus Horrman's private office.

Horrman was in no pleasant mood. Within a short period he had lost $34,000 in a holdup, and a further $6,250, discounting $35,000 of his choicest notes to obtain currency from Cyrus K. Lockridge with which to pay off clamoring depositors. What was even worse, in two days that same Lockridge would become co-owner of the bank and Horrman had come to thoroughly detest the big bland Chicago speculator. A dozen times he had regretted his impetuosity at Bubbling Spring.

"Well?" he snapped as Pollard stood awkwardly by his desk, twiddling the package of bills.

"I am completely bewildered, Mr. Horrman."

The banker eyed his clerk sharply, "Shortage?" His voice was razor-edged.

"No, but we are paying out looted currency!"

Horrman swung around in his chair, shrewd eyes searching Pollard's sunken features. He sniffed, "You haven't been drinking, I hope?"

The clerk flushed. "Nothing but coffee," he returned, with some asperity.

"Then talk sensibly! How could we pay out currency that was stolen?"

Pollard held out the package. "You see that mark?"

Horrman eyed a yellow smudge that stained one edge of the neatly packed wad and nodded brusquely.

"That's mustard! Before the holdup I was in the habit of dropping my sandwiches in the cash drawer when a customer entered. Then I noticed that mustard from them had soiled some of the currency. I ceased the practice and very carefully wiped out the drawer." His voice rose with excitement, "The cash drawer was completely emptied by the robbers — yet there is a package of the original bills!"

Horrman chewed his thin lips, regarding the stain with close attention now. "You are positive nothing was left?"

"I'd stake my life on it, Mr. Horrman!"

"A smear of mustard could easily have been overlooked when you cleaned the drawer."

The clerk pulled out his handkerchief, spread it and held it up by two corners. "I have just wiped out the drawer again — not a trace!"

Horrman sat in frowning silence, bony fingers interlocked and lips pursed as he weighed staggering implications. Again, he studied the yellow stain.

"Sit down, Pollard!" His irritability had vanished. "You are positive that this package was received from Lockridge?"

"Certainly! There is nothing but his currency in the drawer. There have been few withdrawals since the — panic."

"Do you realize what this means?"

"There is only one conclusion, Mr. Horrmon. He returned our own funds, for which we paid him, dollar for dollar."

"Plus an outrageous premium!"

The banker rose, glared at the package, moved restlessly to the window. "This is monstrous, incredible!" he muttered. "There must be some simple explanation." He stepped back to the desk, dropped the stained package of greenbacks into a drawer, "We must give this further thought, Pollard. Naturally, you will observe the utmost secrecy regarding our suspicions. And — er — I appreciate your acumen!"

"Thank you, Mr. Horrman!" said the clerk dryly, and withdrew.

The banker had a logical mind and the capacity of analyzing a problem without allowing his conclusions to be clouded by personal prejudice. Alone, he considered the stained bills calmly and deliberately and came to the conclusion that his clerk was — in some way — mistaken. It was unthinkable that Cyrus K. Lockridge, much as he disliked the slick, swaggering speculator, could be tied in with a gang of renegades. Moreover, Lockridge had tried to prevent the holdup, had warned him of remarks he had overheard in The Double Eagle and had even joined in repulsing the robbers. But for a mischance, every one would have been killed and the loot recovered. Horrman slid open the desk drawer and eyed the stain again. A smudge of mustard! Pollard always ate his midday meal at his desk. The mustard could have been transferred to the bills in many ways — a smear on his fingers, a blob spilling off a sandwich, a sandwich placed thoughtlessly upon a package of bills. Unconsciously, through force of habit, the clerk might even have dropped a sandwich into the drawer since the holdup. No, decided the banker, Pollard's suspicions were too fantastic to be taken seriously.

Annoyed at himself for becoming excited over what was plainly an impossibility, he flung the package back into the drawer again with disgust. And he mentally awarded the clerk a demerit for failing to restrain an overvivid imagination.

The following afternoon the bank opened a new account. Edgington-Tailborne, spruce as usual in silk shirt and tailored riding breeches, breezed through the doorway, affixed his monocle and beamed affably at the cashier. "So this is the jolly old bank! I am Reginald Edgington-Tailborne, manager of the ACC. I wish to deposit a spot of cash. We have an account at the county seat but, after all, one should patronize local industries, what?" He opened his wallet and abstracted some loose bills, "This is merely a token payment, a starter, shall we say?"

Pollard made the necessary notations, then stepped towards the office. "Mr. Horrman makes it a point to greet all new depositors!"

"Charmed!" drawled the Dude.

The clerk ushered him inside. Horrman rose and extended his hand, "I recently purchased some of your land, Mr. Tailborne," he observed.

"Edgington-Tailborne," corrected the Dude gently, "Hyphened!" He dropped onto a chair, stretched out his long legs and achieved an attitude of complete relaxation, the monocle still glinting in his right eye.

"Mr. Edgington-Tailborne," repeated the banker with obvious self-repression. Didn't he have enough on his mind, he thought irately, without having this clothes-dummy thrust upon him?

"So Cyrus K. Lockridge changed his mind about the thousand acres," drawled the Dude. "I understood it was to be dedicated to the public, as a park. Rather superfluous, don't you think, with a million empty acres around?"

Horrman snapped to attention. "Public Park! You probably are not aware that the Chicago & Western railroad has floated a bond issue to construct a line through Vulture Valley, connecting with the Pacific Coast. That land is valuable, Mr. Tail — Edgington-Tailborne."

"Stuff and nonsense!" chided his visitor amiably. "I thought that bankers were hard-headed blighters, men of iron, doncher know, and proof against fantastic rumors."

"This, sir, chances to be a fact," brindled Horrman.

The Englishman languidly drew out a leather wallet, withdrew a folded telegraph blank, smoothed out the yellow sheet and handed it to Horrman. With growing horror, the banker read:

REPLYING TO YOUR WIRE. RUMORS DEVOID OF FOUNDATION. NEITHER WP NOR OURSELVES PLAN EXTENSION THRU VULTURE VALLEY. QUIT DREAMING AND TEND TO YOUR COWS.

YOUR UNCLE
ERNEST.

"Who — who is your Uncle Ernest?" There was a quaver in the banker's voice.

"Chairman of the Board, Chicago & Western Railroad, old bean!"

Edgington-Tailborne eyed the little man at the desk curiously. Strange fellow, he thought, seemed to have difficulty in breathing. Maybe another lunger banished into the desert. Horrman pushed back his chair and achieved a ghastly parody of a smile, "You must excuse me, I have to leave for Apache City — immediately."

Bill Gotch, sheriff of Apache County, greeted Justus Horrman with the blend of easy affability and naive deference that marks a good politician. He was a heavy-set man, running to fat, with tolerant lips and shrewd eyes. Though he never forgot the existence of a ballot-box, Gotch was a square-shooter and a good lawman.

He settled his weight into his swivel chair and heard the banker's outraged story from beginning to end with no more than an occasional sympathetic grunt.

"What do you want me to do, Mr. Horrman?" he inquired at the end of the recital.

"Arrest the infamous crook!" grated the banker.

"Sure!" agreed Gotch easily. "You sign a complaint and we'll pick up the jasper."

"And the money he wheedled out of me by false pretenses?"

"Wal, now," the sheriff eyed the fly-specked calendar on the wall, "That would be a matter f'r the judge."

Limpy braced Cyrus K. Lockridge at a poker table in The Double Eagle thirty minutes before the stage pulled out. Gotch stood by the bar, hand dangling over a gun butt, while another deputy loitered by the batwings. If the hombre was as slick as Justus Horrman claimed, decided the sheriff, he couldn't afford to take chances.

Sam, who could spot a lawman as quickly as a hawk could a chicken, saw the odds were too great and went quietly. Mentally, he made a resolution never to take a seat that faced a side wall again.

The sheriff and his aide escorted him to the county seat, and the three had the interior of the stage to themselves. Seldom had the lawmen enjoyed the company of a more agreeable travelling companion. The prisoner's amazement when he learned the charge was obtaining money through misrepresentation and fraud, and conspiracy to rob a bank, was obviously genuine. He offered no alibis, he just laughed. The lawmen had difficulty in persuading him that the arrest was authentic and he was not witnessing a manifestation of Western humor. Later, Gotch confided to his deputy that it bore all the earmarks of a trumped-up case and Horrman would be hard-put to make his charges stick. "Sure," agreed the deputy, "Everyone in the Valley knows Horrman is a money-grubbing old stinker who'd skin a louse and send its hide to market."

Meanwhile the prisoner was lodged in jail, enjoyed the best of food, supplied — at his expense — by a nearby restaurant, and proved to two horse-thieves in the next cell that their knowledge of poker was strictly elementary.

The third day, arrival of Horrman with a lawyer broke up a game of seven-up that the prisoner was playing through the bars with his jailer. A trifle shame-faced, the jailer, an alkalied old-timer, slipped the greasy pack into a pants pocket and unlocked the door of the cell.

Shaking with fury at the sight of the prisoner, Horrman entered with his legal counselor, a florid gentleman with a melodious voice and an aroma of stale whisky. Legal talent in Apache City was not plentiful.

"You'll get a life sentence for this, Lockridge!" gritted the banker.

Sam dropped upon his bunk and eyed the waspy little man with amusement. "My suit for defamation of character and false arrest will probably cost you plenty," he observed, biting off the end of a cigar. " 'Let your talk be worthy of belief.' " He smiled good-naturedly at the lawyer, "From the Latin!"

"First you delude me with a slick story that a railroad will be built through Vulture Valley," stormed Horrman, "Then you rob my bank and sell me my own securities — at a premium!"

"These are allegations," put in the lawyer smoothly, "which we intend later to substantiate in court." He checked another outburst by his client with a warning gesture. "However, if you make full restitution of the money of which my client has allegedly been defrauded, he authorizes me to inform you that the charges will not be unduly pressed."

The prisoner lit his cigar. "In plain English, friend counselor," he returned blandly, "your case is weak and you are anxious to compromise."

"Weak!" frothed Horrman, "Why, you crook, didn't you sell me a thousand acres of bare range, worth perhaps $500, for $15,000? Didn't you trick me out of a half-interest in my bank for a section of worthless land, with some miserable buildings? Didn't you palm off the bank's own looted funds upon me for the cream of my notes?" He drew a deep breath. "— and discounted 25%?" He spluttered off into silence while Sam regarded his flushed features and puffed his cigar.

The horse-thieves, swarthy, hard-bitten fellows, hunkered in their cell, following the play. The jailer lounged in the doorway of the cell, a chaw bulging his leathery cheek, missing not a word.

"Now you listen to me, gentlemen!" smiled Sam. "I received what I regarded as authentic information that the Chicago & Western Railroad was laying steel through Vulture Valley. I am a speculator! I purchased land, I paid for surveys. You, friend Horrman, prevailed upon me to deed you a half-interest in my holdings, which I did — for a half-interest in your puny bank. You begged for my ACC option, which I assigned to you." He spread his hands, "Is that fraud? Am I at fault if the railroad changes its plans? As for the bank loot," he chuckled. "I have never heard a more ridiculous story. I warn you of the pending holdup. I fight the thieves. I save you from bankruptcy. What thanks do I receive?" His arm circled dramatically, "A cell!" He paused, then smiled sadly, "I am not vindictive, even though I may be the victim of this terrible, this unthinkable, miscarriage of justice. 'The wisest of the wise, may err.' From the Greek, gentlemen! Withdraw the charges and I will relinquish my interest in The Valley Bank. I have no use for such a piddling enterprise! But press them if you wish, friend Justus, and be damned to you!"

"What jury could withstand this man?" thought the lawyer. He cleared his throat in the silence that succeeded Sam's peroration, "So that is your final word?"

"Before I speak my final word," came back the prisoner with cutting emphasis, "That wretched little penny-pincher, that stingy skinful of rapacity, that maggot wriggling in his rotten gold, will have much less than he has now. Please go, gentlemen, before the aroma becomes overpowering!"

Froth bubbled upon Horrman's lips. His lawyer took his arm and gently led him from the cell.

Cyrus K. Lockridge spent two more days in pleasant idleness, while the banker and his lawyer held protracted conferences in Horrman's quarters, located in a shabby house on a side street that carried the sign, "Mrs. Murphy — Clean Rooms." The Western House was infinitely more attractive and provided a good table, but its rates were high — too high for Justus Horrman's taste.

By the end of the second day the banker was approaching nervous prostration, but he still refused to yield to his legal advisor's pleas that he compromise. "Mr. Horrman!" pleaded the lawyer, at the end of a protracted session, "Cannot you realize that the evidence against this man is slight, so slight that I very much doubt if we can obtain a conviction. We may suspect, we may even know, but we cannot prove! Should Lockridge be acquitted, you will not only lose all, but you will face a damaging suit. Let us view the matter like sensible men — is not half a loaf far better than none?"

Bleary-eyed and worn from worry and loss of sleep, the banker still shook his head stubbornly.

The next afternoon, however, Montgomery L. Wordsworth, the lawyer, again broke up an engrossing card game in the jail.

"Mr. Lockridge," he said smoothly, "my client is a lenient man, and furthermore he wishes to return to his business. He is willing to withdraw all charges if you will relinquish your half-interest in his bank and return the notes."

"Brother," smiled Sam, and the devil danced in his eyes, "I have agreed to return to Justus his half-interest. As for the notes, I paid him good money for them. But we will let Lady Luck decide. I will cut the deck for the notes — high man takes all."

The lawyer swallowed, "Do you mean to suggest that we decide the ownership of notes worth $35,000 by a mere turn of the cards?"

"One cut — high man takes all!" returned Sam casually.

"My client will never agree!"

" 'Chance is but a nickname of Providence,' brother. From the French!"

"Have you no other compromise to suggest?"

"Nothing!" declared the confidence man firmly. "Tomorrow I hire me a lawyer and we quit talking. 'Talk does not cook rice.' From the Chinese, counselor!"

Four men sat around the scratched and spur-scarred desk in the sheriff's office. The desk was bare except for a loose sheaf of notes, pinned together. Bill Gotch broke open a new deck of cards, shuffled them, set them face downwards beside the notes. "This ain't strictly according to the statutes, gents," he commented affably, "but it strikes me as being a mighty sensible way to settle an argument. Afore you cut, let's get the matter straight. Mr. Horrman here withdraws all charges against Mr. Lockridge, who agrees to let bygones be bygones. You gents cut once apiece. Ace is high. High man takes the pot, meaning the notes. Correct?"

"Exactly!" approved Montgomery L. Wordsworth, the lawyer, "All the necessary papers have been signed."

Horrman said nothing. He had obviously not slept well. Lips twitching, fingers nervously plucking at his coat, he was staring as if fascinated at the notes.

The sheriff shuffled again, "Wal, cut your luck, gents!"

"After you, Justus!" said Sam sonorously, rolling an unlighted cigar between his lips.

Horrman's right hand dabbed out, hesitated, then jerked back. "You first!" His voice was a husky whisper.

Carelessly, Sam reached out and neatly divided the pack. Turned the cards and displayed his cut — the three of spades.

Gotch whistled. Sam smiled. A wild light gleamed in the banker's bloodshot eyes. Like a claw, fingers hooked, his right hand clutched at the stack, fumbled, lifted and turned. Every eye focussed upon the card that showed in his palm — It was the deuce of clubs!

"I'll be goshdarned!" ejaculated Gotch.

Horrman stared at the deuce as though it were a rattlesnake about to strike.

"Wal, I guess they're yours, Lockridge," drawled the sheriff.

Sam said nothing. He pulled a block of stinkers from his pocket, struck one and touched it to the tip of his cigar. Then he casually held the match to the sheaf of notes.

The sheriff's hand darted out to extinguish the blaze. Sam swept it aside, "Friend sheriff," he said firmly, "I reserve the right to do what I wish with my own property."

Before the horrified lawyer, astonished sheriff and stricken banker, the paper blazed and the notes curled into blackened embers.

"Thirty-five thousand dollars!" shrieked Horrman. "Mine!" He jerked erect, clawing at his throat, shuddered, went down in a heap on the plank floor.

Sheriff Gotch heaved to his feet and knelt beside the crumpled form in the shiny serge suit. The lawyer pulled a flask out of a hip pocket.

Gotch rose heavily and dusted off the knees of his pants. "Save it!" he said curtly, "He's daid!"

CHAPTER NINETEEN

DEPUTY SHERIFF Leeman swung his stiff leg awkwardly across his sweated pony and stepped down at the smooth hitch rail in front of the county courthouse. When he opened the door of the sheriff's office the draft whirled blackened fragments of paper across the floor.

Sheriff Gotch, feet on the desk, the *Apache County Times* spread carefully over his face to form a rampart against the buzzing flies, snored peacefully.

Limpy slammed the door. As he hoped, the sheriff stirred, jerked the newspaper aside and turned his head. "There's no peace f'r wicked," he grumbled. "Howdy, Limpy!"

"Stage is stalled this side of Pacheco Creek," volunteered the deputy, "Axle broke!"

"You didn't swallow dust f'r forty miles tuh tell me that!"

"Nope — brought a picture along." The deputy dug a creased reward notice out of a pants pocket, set it on the desk beside the sheriff's boots.

With a yawn, Gotch reached out and picked it up. It carried the reproduction of a hawk-nosed man with piercing eyes and heavy jaw. Beneath, in black capitals, was printed:

$1,000 REWARD

is offered for information leading to the recapture of Samuel Shortridge, Alias Slick Sam, who escaped from Yuma Penitentiary May 16. Height 6' 2"; weight 246 lbs; age 39. Hair black; dark eyes, deepset. This man is a notorious bank robber and confidence man. Usually operates alone. Well educated. May be disguised.

James Farlow,

Warden,

Yuma Territorial Penitentiary.

"Wal?" inquired the sheriff, "The hombre hanging out in Powwow?"

"Nope, you picked him up. He's jailed — right now."

Gotch's boots hit the floor with a thud, "Hell, it ain't — it ain't Cyrus K. Lockridge?"

"Thet's the gent," supplied Limpy, "with a spade beard. It hit me like a ton of rock when I was wolfing my flapjacks this A.M. Guess I get a slice of thet thousand, Bill?"

"Hell-and-blazes! He skipped, Limpy! Horrman withdrew all charges. We had quite a session. Lockridge burned $35,000 of the old tightwad's notes and Horrman dropped dead — from shock."

"Mebbe he's still around town?"

"Nope, he pulled out on the stage."

Harrigan hunched on a stool in Ruby's Pie Shop and regarded the dregs in his coffee cup with lack-luster eyes. A portion of pie stood untouched on the plate beside it. He could see the gates of Yuma looming close and could almost feel the black horror of the Snake Pen. An hour before he had ridden into town, eager to break the monotony of a week's grind, combing the foothills gathering a beef shipment. No sooner had he tied his pony than a garrulous townsman had broken the big news — Cyrus K. Lockridge, the flash Chicago business man, had ben arrested by Limpy Leeman in The Double Eagle, while Sheriff Gotch and another deputy had hustled him into the Apache City stage. Wild rumors were circulating — Lockridge had engineered the bank holdup; he was an escaped convict; there was an accomplice, suspected of murdering Droop-Eye, whose arrest was expected any time. The whole town was agog.

This was it, reflected the Turtle foreman somberly. They'd put the finger on him next. Bill Moggs knew he was down to Droop-Eye's shack the day before the body was found, and Moggs saved little of his breath for panting. There was nothing, the rider pondered, that he could do about it except high-tail. It was that or Yuma, and he'd sooner rot in boothill than the Snake Pen.

"Say, what's got into you, Yuma?" Ruby refilled his cup. "You act like you ordered your coffin. And what's wrong with that pie?"

"I jest ain't hungry," he replied spiritlessly and pushed the plate aside.

"Did you hear they got Whitey in jail for —"

"I been lookin' for you, Harrigan!" The forman slipped sideways off his stool and whirled as Limpy's harsh voice rasped from the doorway. As he swung around, his right hand snaked down to the butt of the six-gun bumping against his hip. The deputy, one hand holding aside the flycurtains, the other on the door jamb, was caught flat-footed. Harrigan's gun leapt up and out.

Behind him, Ruby grabbed the uncaten pie. Her arm swung. As the gun spat fire and thunder, the portion of pie, with a juicy squish, flattened against the side of Harrigan's face. Deflected, the slug whined across Main Street. Before the astonished rider could thumb again, the deputy's forty-five was aligned on his belt buckle. "Stretch, you crazy maverick!" he grunted.

Gun levelled, the lawman moved close, twisted the smoking iron from Harrigan's grasp. Under the goad of the deputy's gun, a goo of piecrust and soft apples plastered over the right side of his face and head, the rider reluctantly raised his hands shoulder high. He stood stiff, eyes hostile, as Ruby rounded the counter and wiped the sticky remnants of the pie off his features with a towel. "Thanks — pard!" he said, with bitter irony.

"Git movin'!" Limpy stepped behind him and nudged him with the gun barrel. "Ef you crave to sprout wings — start something!"

The prisoner dragged his feet across Main Street, crossed the plankwalk and entered the law shack, the deputy stumping behind.

"Rest yore legs!" invited Limpy, nodding at a chair. He slid open a drawer of his desk, brought out a bottle, "Try a snort," he invited, "Yore as jumpy as a grasshopper."

"You don't have to butter me," came back the other shortly, "What's the charge?"

"Charge!" Limpy's gaunt features wrinkled into something that resembled a grin, "there ain't no charge."

"How come you gathered me in?" scowled the prisoner.

"Jest craved to tell yuh, yore clear!"

"Of Droop-Eye's killing?"

Limpy dropped into a chair and fished out the makin's. He seemed to be enjoying himself. "Heck, I picked up Whitey f'r that this A.M."

Harrigan's puzzled gaze was riveted on the lawman, "Then what am I clear of? Not — not Harry Hartstone's murder?" His voice was hesitant with suspense.

"Sure!" Limpy built his smoke, "Whitey cracked wide open."

"Ther's a dozen could swear he was in the saloon when Harry was plugged."

"Hobble yore hawses," grunted the deputy, "and bend yore ears."

With a deliberation that rasped Harrigan's tight-strung nerves like a jagged knife edge, he lit the cylinder of tobacco and took a leisurely draw. "Whitey give Cheyenne Dan $1,000 tuh down Hartstone and Chunky Nabor $500 tuh plant yore gun and swear you plugged him. Cheyenne pulled his freight, but Chunky braced Whitey for more dinero. Seems like the pair was tied up in a rustling deal, too. So Whitey laid f'r the jasper, and Chunky got his'n. The rattlesnake sicked me onto you, claimed he lamped you and Chunky augurin' down by the creek. Thet's why I picked you up." Limpy eased his stiff leg.

"Getting back to Hartstone. Droop-Eye was sleepin' off a drunk in the alley. With Cheyenne out of town and Chunky dead, Whitey figgered he was safe, 'til you drifted down to Droop-Eye's shack. I was in The Double Eagle when Bill Moggs spilt the news. All through I figgered there was something crooked about your conviction. Yore sort don't kill f'r dinero. Wal, Whitey was playing solitaire and he misplaced a card when Bill Moggs talked. Now it ain't customary f'r Whitey to misplace cards, which give me a hunch. I kept cases on Droop-Eye's cabin. Sure enough, after sundown a gent comes bustin' through the brush and slides into the shack. He leaves later and I dogged him back tuh town. It was Whitey. At sunup I looked the shack over — and you know what I found! Then the sheriff pulls me into Apache City on this Lockridge deal and I figgers Whitey u'll keep."

The deputy drew complacently on his smoke, "I braced him this morning and he talked — plenty... with a little persuasion!"

Harrigan was following every word with rapt attention. "How come you laid off when you cornered me in Ruby's cabin?"

"Whitey give me thet lead, claimed there was a stranger bunkin' up with Ruby. Wal, I figgered the gal knew more 'n I did and mebbe I should let you run around awhiles."

"It still don't make sense," interjected Harrigan, with creased brow. "What did Whitey have against Harry that he'd pay $1,500 to wipe him out?"

"You forget the $20,000 Hartstone carried in his jeans!"

"So that's where it went!"

"Pollard took $3,300."

"The bank clerk?" Harrigan's head was whirling.

"So Whitey claims. I ain't got Pollard's story yet. What say we brace the gent?" Limpy tossed the rider his gun. Together, they left the shack and angled across street towards the bank, checking to avoid the dust stirred by two riders. It was Edgington-Tailborne and Joan Findley, riding close, They were too interested in each other to notice the men afoot.

Shoulders rounded, the clerk was bent over his ledger. He carefully stuck his pen in the inkwell, stepped off the high stool and stood patiently awaiting them behind the wicket.

Both men stepped up to the counter and stared at the hollow-cheeked, seedy clerk without speaking. Who would be less likely to plan Harry Hartstone's death than this weak, stoop-shouldered townsman, thought Harrigan.

Pollard's mild eyes regarded first one, then the other. He cleared his throat nervously, "What do you want, gentlemen?"

"You!" said Limpy harshly, "Accessory to the murder of Harry Hartstone — Whitey spilled his guts!"

"Would you," asked Pollard diffidently, "be so kind as to step into the office?"

"Sure!" said the deputy, climbing across the counter with surprising agility for a lame man, "After you!"

The three filed into the office that had been Justus Horrman's. The clerk sank onto a chair by the window. Limpy squatted on the desk, eying him closely. Harrigan stood by the door.

Pollard pulled out a handkerchief and dabbed his forehead.

"Start talkin'!" grated Limpy.

The clerk smiled apologetically, "You may not believe me, officer, but this is a relief. The memory of that crime has tortured me, day and night."

"How come you got tied up in it?"

"It's a long, long story."

"Spill it!"

"Four years ago, gentlemen, I was chief clerk for the United Trust Company, New York. I enjoyed an excellent salary. I had a comfortable home, a good wife and two fine children. Then misfortune struck me. I became sick. The doctors diagnosed tuberculosis. They said my only chance for life was to move to a hot, dry climate. They suggested Arizona.

"Medical treatment had exhausted my savings. We sold our home. I bought a small cottage for my wife and children, left them the balance after I had purchased a ticket West and taken a few dollars for expenses. It was understood that when I obtained a satisfactory position I would send for them and we would make a new home in Arizona." Pollard smiled wanly. "What is there for a bank clerk, dying of T.B., in Arizona? I wandered from town to town seeking a position, in vain. My money ran out. I was reduced to eating from garbage cans. At last I obtained this position. The salary was so small I could scarcely support myself. I could send little back to my family. My wife wrote that she was expecting another child and she needed money. Then she was taken to the hospital. There were bills, bills, bills!" The clerk paused, closed his eyes and continued drearily, "The inevitable occurred. William Hartstone's account had been dormant for months. He was dead and his estate in the hands of the court. I forged checks against that account. As the months, years passed my peculations amounted to thousands. I do not excuse them. I had a wife, baby and two children depending upon me for the necessities of life.

"Then the court awarded Harry Hartstone his uncle's estate, including a $20,000 bank balance — and the account was $3,300 short! I knew I could hide my — borrowing — no longer.

"I am not a drinking man, but the evening of the day Hartstone drew his $20,000 I went down to the saloon. Drink loosened my tongue. Whitey, the manager, was sympathetic. I told him Hartstone had drawn $20,000 and I faced exposure and disgrace. He asked if Hartstone was carrying the money. I said yes. He wanted to know what I needed to cover up. I told him $3,300.

"That night Hartstone was shot and $3,300 in greenbacks was handed me when the bank opened the next day. That is all!"

Harrigan broke a silence that clothed the room like a cold shroud, "So Whitey framed me f'r $16,700!"

Limpy's expressionless eyes dwelt on the wilted form beneath the window. "You got a gun around here?"

"Mr. Horrman always kept a .45 in the top drawer of his desk."

The deputy pulled out the drawer and peered inside, "Yep!" He eased himself off the desk, slid a .45 slug from a loop of his gun belt. "Ketch!" he grated, and tossed it to the clerk. "Le's go, Harrigan!"

"Don't that beat all creation!" exclaimed Harrigan, as they again plugged across Main Street. A gun boomed in the bank behind them. He threw a quick glance at Limpy's bleak features, "Reckon Pollard used that shell!"

"I guess so!" returned the deputy, without interest. "Le's have a drink!"

CHAPTER TWENTY

SHADOWS lay long across Main Street and store windows glowed yellow. It had been a heavy day for Harrigan. He left Limpy in The Double Eagle and stepped out into the quietness of the darkening street. His mind was still in a ferment, he wanted to be alone — to think. Even now it was hard to believe that he was a free man, free for ever from the threat of return to Yuma. As he drifted aimlessly along the plankwalk, his thoughts wandered to the mild, hollow-cheeked man who had been the cause of it all, now lying dead in the bank. He thought of a woman left alone, with a baby and two children, waiting in a far-off city for money that would never come. Now she would be more alone than ever.

He found himself standing outside the rock-and-adobe bank, dark and silent as a tomb. He pushed back the swinging door and entered the gloomy premises. His footsteps echoed hollowly as he crossed the polished floor and quietly eased into the private office. A form was blotched below the window. He struck a match, and quickly dropped it — the remains of Pollard's face did not make a pretty sight. A gun lay loosely in the dead man's right hand and a photograph was clutched in his left. Harrigan struck another match and eyed the photograph — a woman, still young, with grave, oval features, was sitting in a chair with a baby on her lap. Beside her, two children were standing, solemn faced. To them, it was plain, this was a great occasion.

The rider fumbled in the dead man's pockets until he found a wallet. In it were letters, with New York postmarks.

Harrigan pushed his head through the flycurtains of Ruby's Pie Shop. "Kin I come in without being crowned with a pie?" he drawled.

"Sure," came back the girl, eyes flashing a welcome, "If you keep your hand off that gun."

She drew him a cup of coffee, "I suppose your appetite doesn't stretch to pie?"

"You jest try me," he grinned, "I could eat a hawse, saddle and all."

When nothing remained of an entire dried apple pie, except crumbs, he pulled a letter out of his pocket and laboriously copied the address at its head upon the back of an envelope.

" 'Member that pack of greenbacks I cached with you?" he queried, "Maybe you'd mail it to that address."

Ruby picked up the envelope and read aloud, "Mrs. Pollard, 2511 Maybury Street, New York. Say — what's doing? Wouldn't that be the bank cashier's wife?"

"Widow," he corrected, "Pollard jest drilled a hole in his conk, f'r good reason." He fished out the photograph, pushed it across to her, "His family — and flat busted!"

"I'll mail it, Yuma," she said softly.

He slid off the stool, lifted his hat from the peg and twiddled it restlessly in his fingers.

Ruby leaned on the counter, "Well, what's itching you now? You sure have no dinero to worry about." There was a roguish light in her dark eyes, "You framing to marry the widow and get a family, ready-made?"

"Dammit, quit riding me!" he spluttered. He moved back to the counter, studiously eying the Stetson that twirled in his nervous fingers. "Bull's got a dandy cabin f'r his foreman, sheet iron stove, mail order suite in the living room, pictures on the walls."

"No bedroom set?" inquired Ruby wickedly.

"Can't you button up?" he blurted, then lapsed into an embarrassed silence.

"Well?" she prompted, and her eyes were soft, "Could he use a married man?"

"That's jest what I was getting around to!" He dropped the hat, reached across the counter and grasped her eagerly, a hand on each shoulder, "You game, Ruby? We'd travel well in double harness."

"Oh, Yuma!"

"Maybe," he glanced around the store uncertainly, "You wouldn't want to leave the business."

"The business!" The tone of Ruby's voice left no doubt as to what she thought of that.

In Cell 2, Main Block, Yuma Territorial Penitentiary, five men stretched listlessly on their bunks, wet with the sweat that stained the straw pallets. The ironbound door grated open. A big man, with a hawk nose, square jaw and neat spade beard, strode in, while a guard slammed the door behind him.

A bull-necked man with bloodshot eyes raised his head incuriously, then sat up with a jerk, "Geehoshaphat! Lamp this, Drago! Slick's back — with a beard!"

"Greetings!" returned the new arrival sonorously. He closed his nostrils significantly with forefinger and thumb of his right hand, and bowed, "I trust that during my absence your conduct has brought honor upon this excellent institution."

"How come they nabbed yuh, Slick?"

"Luck is a jade, her name is deceit; a wanton maid, a flagrant cheat; by her betrayed, I met defeat." Sam smiled sadly, "That, gentlemen, is original!"